THE RIPPER

Morning was not too far off, she was a block away from home, and the street ahead of her was empty until a large, dark figure stepped out onto the path.

"Hey!" she said, stopping short.

"Hello, luv," the man said. "Got time for me?"

She waved him away and said, "I'm through for the night, friend. You should have caught me a little earlier in the evening. Why not try tonight?"

"Tonight won't do, I'm afraid."

He had a very cultured voice, with some kind of accent, and he seemed clean. Too bad she was too tired, even for one more customer.

"Why not?" she asked.

"I'm afraid you won't be alive by then," he said, taking a step toward her.

"Wha—" she said, but that was all she had time for . . .

THE GUNSMITH

165

THE DENVER RIPPER

J. R. ROBERTS

JOVE BOOKS, NEW YORK

THE DENVER RIPPER

A Jove Book / published by arrangement with
the author

PRINTING HISTORY
Jove edition / September 1995

ISBN: 0-515-11703-X

A JOVE BOOK®
Jove Books are published by The Berkley Publishing Group,
200 Madison Avenue, New York, New York 10016.
JOVE and the "J" design are trademarks
belonging to Jove Publications, Inc.

PRINTED IN THE UNITED STATES OF AMERICA

10 9 8 7 6 5 4 3 2 1

PROLOGUE

The man stood in the shadows and watched the woman walk down the street. She was perfect, exactly the kind he liked. She was young and pretty, and she plied her trade on the streets. It was coming on early morning now, and she quickened her pace, apparently in a hurry to get home. She was coming toward him, though, so all he had to do was wait for her.

Come to Poppa . . .

Jacy Hastings was exhausted. She'd had a good night, but all that meant was that she'd made a lot of money by being with a lot of men, and she was tired. Three of the men had been dirty, and smelly, and now she felt the same way. All she wanted to do was get home and take a nice hot bath before going to sleep.

At twenty-five Jacy had been working the streets

of Denver for the past five years. She knew she couldn't do it much longer, though. Another couple of years and her looks would start to fade. At thirty she'd look forty. She knew a lot of women who it had already happened to, and she didn't want it to happen to her. When she was thirty she wanted to look thirty.

She was a block away from home and the street ahead of her was empty until a large, dark figure stepped out into her path.

"Hey!" she said, stopping short.

"Hello, luv," the man said. "Got time for me?"

She waved him away and said, "I'm through for the night, friend. You should have caught me a little earlier in the evening. Why not try tonight?"

"Tonight won't do, I'm afraid."

He had a very cultured voice, with some kind of accent, and he seemed clean. Too bad she was too tired, even for one more customer.

"Why not?" she asked.

"I'm afraid you won't be alive by then," he said, taking a step toward her.

"Wha—" she said, but that was all she had time for as a sharp blade pierced her in the side, driving any further words and all the air from her lungs.

The man grabbed her around the shoulders and pulled her into the alley with him. He forced her to the ground and went to work with the blade. Mercifully, the first thrust had killed Jacy Hastings, and she didn't feel anything else after that. . . .

ONE

Clint felt a tinge of excitement as he got off the train at the Denver railway station. He had not been to Denver in some time, nor had he seen his old friend Bat Masterson in a while. To be doing both at one time was something he was looking forward to.

It felt odd to be without his big black gelding, Duke, but he had decided to leave the horse behind this trip. In Labyrinth at least Duke would be getting some exercise. Here in Denver he most likely would have ended up standing in some livery most of the time.

He picked up his carpetbag from the platform and walked into the station. Although Bat knew he was coming, Clint did not expect his friend to meet him at the station, so he was surprised when he saw Bat Masterson coming toward him with a big smile on his face. He was resplendent in a dark suit, boiled white shirt, and a bowler hat. He had even taken to carrying a silver-tipped cane.

"Clint, you old dog."

Masterson, shorter but stockier than Clint, caught him in a bear hug that all but squeezed the air entirely from his lungs.

Clint dropped his bag and, even in the crowded station, unabashedly hugged his friend back, so strong was the bond of their friendship.

"It's good to see you, Bat."

"And you, by God it is."

The two friends regarded each other critically and came to the same conclusion. The years had been kind to them.

"You've put on some weight," Clint said, patting Bat's middle.

"That's my prosperity bulge," Bat said. "You'd get one, too, if you stayed put in one place long enough."

"Denver's your place now, huh?"

"And why not? I've got my own newspaper column and now I own a sports club."

"A sports club? When did that happen?"

"I'll tell you about it on the way," Bat said, picking Clint's bag up.

"I've got to get to a hotel—"

"Nonsense. You're staying at my place."

"Is it big enough?"

"My club, Clint," Bat said. "You'll stay at the sports club."

Clint knew that Bat had started writing a newspaper column, but the news of this "club" was brand-new.

"Well, let's get started, then," he said. "I've got to hear this."

•   •   •

During the ride Bat explained to Clint that he was now part owner of the Olympic Club, a men's sports club where he often put on professional fights. He was also the sports editor for a newspaper called *George's Weekly*, and had a weekly column in that same newspaper.

"You've turned into an entrepreneur, Bat," Clint said.

"Something like that."

"I knew about the writing, but how did the fight club come about?"

"That is not a happy story, my friend, but . . ." Bat looked out the window of the cab. ". . . we still have some time, so . . ."

Bat told Clint how he and a man named Otto Floto, who was also the sports editor of the *Denver Post*, had planned to open a club together, called the Colorado Club. They had a falling-out, however, when Floto managed to grab controlling interest—and, in fact, sole interest—in what was supposed to be a joint venture, thereby forcing Bat out.

"So you opened your own club?"

"You're damned right I did. I secured the old Haymarket Theater and turned it into the Olympic Club. My club will make Floto's club look pathetic! He can't possibly get the kind of fights I can."

"And I imagine the two of you have something to say about each other in your columns?"

Bat cleared his throat and said, "From time to time, yes."

Before they could go any further they arrived at the corner of Sixteenth and Market streets, where Bat's club was. As they got out Clint looked up at the brick building and saw the faded lettering on the side that said ACADEMY OF MUSIC.

"I'm still having it worked on. That faded lettering will be gone by the time my architects are done." Bat said this proudly.

"Bat, where did you get the money for this kind of venture?"

"Investors, my friend," Bat said, rubbing his hands together, "investors. In fact, I thought about asking you to invest, but I decided to keep our friendship apart from business."

"A wise idea," Clint agreed.

Bat clapped Clint on the back and said, "Come on inside and I'll show you to your room. After that we can go and get something to drink."

"And eat," Clint said.

"Oh yes," Bat said, waving his hand, "and that, too. We might even be able to scare up a poker game, huh? What do ya say?"

"I say food first, and we can talk about the rest later."

"Good enough!" Bat said. "Come this way."

TWO

Bat showed Clint through the massive lobby to a curved staircase leading to the second floor.

"I've had the second floor converted to guest rooms and, of course, my own room. The downstairs has been renovated and is now a gentlemen's bar and restaurant."

"And the fights?"

"In the theater," Bat said. "I didn't touch that, except to take out enough seats for a ring to fit. I even left the stage as is. You never know when you might need one."

Bat stopped at one of the doors and threw it open theatrically.

"This is your room. Best room in the house—next to mine."

Clint entered ahead of Bat, who followed with his bag. It was a beautiful room, decorated in deep maroons and greens. There was a chest of drawers, a bureau, a sofa, a cherry wood writing desk, and a huge bed.

"I'll leave you to get freshened up. Through there you'll find modern facilities." Bat was obviously very proud of his establishment.

"I can't wait to see the downstairs."

"I'll wait for you in the bar," Bat said. "Half an hour?"

"Or less," Clint said. "I'm hungry."

"Good. You'll be a good judge of my kitchen."

Clint stared at his friend and shook his head.

"What?" Bat asked.

"I just can't see you as a settled-in businessman," Clint said. "How long do you think this is going to last?"

"As long as I make money at it," Bat said. "You get changed and I'll meet you downstairs."

Impulsively Bat crossed the room and took hold of Clint's arm.

"Damn, but it's good to see you."

"You, too, Bat."

Bat nodded, squeezed his arm, and left. Clint looked around again, shaking his head. The fact that Bat owned this whole place was something that was going to take getting used to. Clint had known Bat to become involved in some dubious business deals—from saloons to managing wrestlers and fighters—but this . . . this was the biggest thing by far that his friend had become involved in, and yet Bat Masterson and entrepreneurship did not seem such an odd couple.

Clint's growling stomach reminded him of his hunger and he decided to do the rest of his thinking while he made use of the modern facilities Bat had spoken of.

When Clint came down the stairs to the lobby he paused a moment to get his bearings. He heard voices to the right and the sound of glasses, dishes, and silverware to his left. He assumed, then, that the bar was to the right and went that way.

As he entered the room he saw Bat standing at the bar with two well-dressed gentlemen, each holding a glass of some sort. Bat had a beer, while the other two men had shot glasses of whiskey. All around the room were small round tables, most of them with men sitting at them. There were no women in sight. Bat Masterson's Olympic Club seemed to be doing a brisk business.

"Clint. Come on over, I want you to meet some people," Bat called out.

Knowing he was the center of attention as he crossed the room, Clint exchanged pleasant nods with some of the people he passed at tables.

"Clint Adams, meet Herbert George, my editor at *George's Weekly.*"

George was an older man in his sixties with a florid face and a potbelly. From the way he was dressed, though, he was obviously very well-off. There was a gold chain hanging from his vest, and Clint was sure that in the vest pocket was a gold watch to go with it.

"Mr. George."

"A pleasure, Mr. Adams. I was just talking to Bat here about the possibility of doing an interview with you while you were here."

"I don't know about that, Mr. George," Clint said.

"There's been quite enough written about me already, I think. Besides, I thought Bat was the sports editor."

"That's just it," George said. "The subject would be sports—or the sporting world which, of course, would include gaming—ah, that is, poker and such. I understand you are quite a gambler."

"I wonder where you got that idea," Clint said, giving his friend the eye.

"Never mind that," Bat said to both of them. "I'll talk to Clint about it later, Herbert. Clint, this other gent here is Frank Quay, a friend of mine from here in Denver."

Quay was closer in age to Bat and Clint, taller and more svelte than the older George. He was similarly dressed, however, and wore a gaudy gold ring on the third finger of his right hand.

"My pleasure, Clint—uh, may I call you Clint?"

"Sure," Clint said, "any friend of Bat's can call me by my first name."

"Well, I guess that means you'll have to keep calling him Mr. Adams, Herbert, huh?" Bat asked.

"What?" the editor said, then got the joke. "Oh, I see. Well, Bat, I have to be going."

"What's your hurry? Stay awhile and have lunch with us."

"I can't," George said. "As you know, there was another woman found this morning."

"Found?" Clint asked.

George looked at him.

"Stabbed to death," George said. "Fourth one in seventeen days. The city is up in arms."

"I guess it would be," Clint said. "I hadn't heard anything about this."

"It's been in most of the major newspapers across the country," George said. "They're either picking it up from us, or the *Post*." Herbert George said the name of the *Denver Post* with obvious distaste. "I've got to get back to the office and make sure we're on top of this. Klinger was supposed to talk to Chief Farley about it."

"Farley?"

"Chief of police," Bat said. "But you didn't come here to hear all about this. Come back later on, Herbert. We'll be trying to get a poker game up for Clint."

George's eyes sparkled as he said, "That would be worth coming back for. I'll try to make it."

As George walked away, Bat said to Clint, "Have a beer and then we'll go and have some lunch. You don't mind if Frank here joins us, do you?"

Frank Quay looked so eager to join them that Clint hadn't the heart to say no.

"Sure, why not," he said. "But first I want that beer."

"You've got it," Bat said, and turned to call the bartender over.

THREE

After a cold beer Bat took Clint and Quay into the dining room, which was more crowded than the bar.

"When they're finished in here they'll all crowd into the bar."

"Are you always this busy, Bat?" Clint asked.

"I wish," Bat said. "There's a fight comin' up in a week. Usually, when there's a fight comin' they crowd in here for lunch and dinner to talk about it—either here or at Floto's place. These killings, though, have got people worried. A lot of these men don't talk about anythin' else, and they don't want to talk about it in front of their wives. Come on, I keep a table in the back."

The table was fitted kitty-corner so that both Bat and Clint were able to sit with a wall behind them. Quay watched them sit and shook his head.

"Frank doesn't know about sitting with your back to the wall," Bat said.

"In my business it's not necessary."

"What business is that, Frank?" Clint asked, figuring that if it was all right for Quay to call him Clint then it was all right for him to return the favor.

"This and that," Quay said evasively.

"This and that" sounded to Clint like the kind of business that had some risks. He'd talk to Bat about it later.

"Steaks are great here," Bat said.

"I'm sold," Clint said.

Bat waved and a waiter who looked about twenty-two appeared.

"Three steak platters, Dave."

"Right, Mr. Masterson."

Clint sat back and surveyed the room. Waiters were crisscrossing back and forth carrying trays, and it looked as if every table was filled.

"Looks like you're doing great here, Bat," Clint said, "even if you're only half this busy most of the time."

"We're doin' all right," Bat said, "but Floto is, too. It's my intention to drive that fat bastard out of business."

"How long do you figure that will take?" Clint asked.

"Unfortunately Floto's got the *Post* behind him. Without them I probably would have had him broke already."

"You'll do it, Bat," Quay said. "He can't last much longer."

"Tell me about these murders, Bat," Clint said.

"They've all been women?"

"What do you want to talk about that for?"

"I'm curious."

"Too curious," Bat said, pointing. "That's always been your problem."

"Well, if that's my only problem I'm doing okay," Clint said.

"Don't you want to talk about the fight that's comin' up?"

"After I hear about the women," Clint said. "Come on, give."

Bat sat back and said, "Ah, there's not much to tell. Four women, all prostitutes, all found on the street, stabbed and cut up."

"Cut up?"

"Pieces taken away," Quay said. "Looks like the killer's collecting chunks of his victims."

"Fingers, you mean like that?"

Bat made a face and looked at Quay.

"Breasts," Quay said, "one girl even had her heart taken."

"Her heart?" Clint asked incredulously.

"See why I don't want to talk about this?" Bat asked. "And look, lunch is comin'."

The young waiter had returned with three steak platters, all cooked rare. He set them down, and the smell started Clint's stomach growling again. The steaks were covered with onions and other vegetables.

"Dave, bring three beers from the bar, will you?" Bat asked.

"Sure, Mr. Masterson."

"You still want to talk about this while we're eating?" Bat asked.

"Oh, I guess it could wait until after we've finished," Clint conceded.

"Okay, then," Bat said, cutting into his steak, "about that fight . . ."

FOUR

During lunch Bat told Clint how he had gotten this fight right out from under Otto Floto's nose. It seemed Floto thought he had the fight all set to appear at his Colorado Club but didn't know that Bat had gone to Chicago to court the name fighter, Jimmy "King of the Ring" King, and his manager, Eddie O'Toole. Once O'Toole and King knew that Bat Masterson wanted them badly enough to come and talk to them, they signed with him.

"Now Floto is toutin' the opponent, Johnny 'Hard Knuckles' Dugan, to beat King."

"Can he?"

"King is in line for a title fight, Clint. There's no way Dugan can beat him."

"There are always ways," Quay said.

"Oh, sure," Bat said, "King could be bought off, but O'Toole would never go for that."

"Maybe King would," Quay said.

16

Bat gave Quay a look of disgust and then said to Clint, "Frank is tryin' to get me to believe that Floto can get to King."

"Like you said," Quay reminded him, "he's got the *Post* behind him. That's a lot of money."

"I talked to both O'Toole and King," Bat said. "Neither one of them is going to be bought."

"I hope you're right," Quay said. He stood up and reached into his pocket, presumably for his wallet.

"Don't take your money out here, Frank," Bat said.

"Thanks for lunch, Bat," Quay said. He looked at Clint and added, "Good to meet you."

"And you."

"See you later, Bat."

"Sure."

As Quay walked away, Bat asked Clint, "You want some coffee?"

"Of course."

He called Dave over to clear the table and bring a pot of coffee.

"Good and strong."

"Yes, sir."

"And bring two pieces of peach pie."

"Right."

As the waiter left, Clint asked, "What does Quay do?"

"He travels, he spends money, he does different things. . . . His old man was rich and left it to Frank when he died a few years back."

"And he doesn't do any work?"

"He works at spendin' money."

"What did he do before that?"

"Drifted, gambled, did some writing, a little bit of

everything. Trouble was, he wasn't good at any of it. He's all right, though."

"You think he's way off about the fight?"

"I think Floto wishes he could buy King and make me look bad, but I don't think it can be done, Clint."

"When does the fighter get here?"

"Couple days before the fight."

"And that's next week?"

"Yep. A week from today."

"A lot can happen between now and then."

"You, too, now?" Bat asked. "Bad enough I got to listen to Frank go on about it—"

"Hey, you wanted to talk about the fight."

"Well, we talked about it."

"Good," Clint said, "then maybe we can get back to talking about the dead women."

"Oh, Jesus, not that. . . . You know what? If you're so damned interested in dead women I'll have a bunch of newspapers brought up to your room so you can read about them? How about that?"

"*George's Weekly?*"

"And the *Post*. You'll get your fill from the both of them. Okay?"

"Okay."

"Ah, here comes the peach pie. Wait until you taste this. . . ."

FIVE

When Bat made a suggestion after lunch about a woman—a *live* woman—Clint said that he thought he should take a bath.

"I'd like to get some rest, too," he said.

"You gettin' old on me, Clint?" Bat asked.

"I'm afraid so, old friend."

Bat touched his own face and said, "I should talk, huh?" He slapped Clint on the back as they both stood up. "Okay, you go get your bath and your rest and meet me down here for dinner. After that we'll see what comes up."

"Sounds good to me, Bat."

"I've got some business to take care of, anyway."

They walked through the lobby together and split up at the stairs. Bat went to his office, which was, he said, behind that staircase, and Clint went up to his room.

• • •

After a bath and a nap Clint woke when there was a knock on his door. He stumbled out of bed and answered it with the sheet wrapped around his waist. The woman standing in the hall looked startled at his appearance. She was young, in her mid-twenties, slender and blond and very pretty.

"Oh, look, honey, tell Bat I appreciate it but I'm really not ready for company right now."

"I beg your pardon?" She looked puzzled now, as well as startled.

"Didn't Bat send you up here?"

"Well, yes, but . . ."

"Maybe you and I can get together later on?"

She frowned and said, "I still don't understand—" She stopped short as something occurred to her. "Wait a minute. Do you think I'm a prostitute?"

"I—well, I, uh . . . aren't you?"

"You've got a lot of nerve, mister." She pointed to the floor and he looked down and saw the stack of papers. "There are the newspapers Mr. Masterson told me to bring to you—and that's all!"

She turned on her heels and stormed off down the hallway.

"Hey, wait . . . I'm sorry, I . . . oh, hell."

He leaned over to pick up the newspapers and as he did he lost the sheet. It fluttered to the floor and he stood in the hallway naked. The woman chose that moment to turn around and look back, and when she saw him she said, "Pig!" and continued on.

"Jesus—" he snapped. He tried to pull the sheet back up and balance the newspapers with one hand but they tumbled back to the floor, this time spreading out in the hall.

"Shit!" He dropped the sheet and started picking

up the newspapers. He tossed them into the room, then grabbed the sheet, went inside, and pulled the door shut behind him.

"Damn it!" He felt like a total fool, looking down at the newspapers that were strewn about. Before picking them up again he pulled on a pair of jeans. He had just buttoned them when there was another knock on the door. He thought it was the girl coming back to tell him what a pig he truly was.

"Listen, I'm sorry—" he said as he swung the door open, but it wasn't the girl, it was Dave, the waiter. He was holding a tray with a pot of coffee and a couple of cups.

"Mr. Masterson thought you might need this, Mr. Adams," the young man said.

"I do need it, Dave. Bring it on in."

Dave came in and set the tray down on top of the cherry wood writing desk.

"Dave, do you know a pretty blond girl, thin, maybe five foot four?"

"That'd be Del Perkins."

"Del?"

"Delilah, but she likes to be called Del."

"What does she do?"

"She works at the *Weekly*."

"You mean the newspaper?"

"That's right. Didn't I see her come up here with those newspapers you wanted?"

"Yeah, she was here," Clint said, feeling foolish again, "just a little before you."

"I thought I saw her coming downstairs. She, uh, looked mad."

"Well," Clint said, "I wasn't at my best when she knocked. What do I owe you for the coffee?"

"Nothin', it's on the house."

"Well, let me give *you* something."

"Can't take it," Dave said, waving his hand. "Mr. Masterson told me if I took a tip from you I better not come back down."

"You do everything Mr. Masterson tells you to do?" Clint asked.

"I sure do."

"Because he's your boss?"

"Oh, no," Dave said. "I respect him. Sure, he gave me a job when I needed it, but ... well, he's Bat Masterson."

"Oh, yeah," Clint said, as Dave went out the door, "he definitely is."

SIX

The coffee was a godsend. Leave it to Bat to know what he'd need when he woke up. He sat at the writing desk with the newspapers and a cup and read the articles on the murders. So far the police had no clues as to who was doing the killing. All of the women had been grabbed on the streets, but then they worked the streets. They were not whores who worked saloons and gambling casinos, they were street whores. They made their living on the streets, but that didn't mean they had to die there, as well.

Four women so far, the most recent having been found—as he heard—that morning. All stabbed and then cut up in some way, mutilated. The police chief, Farley, was predicting a quick arrest, but Clint noticed that he predicted that at the end of every article, after every murder.

Clint also noticed that there was a columnist on the *Weekly* named Earl Klinger, who, after the third murder, called for the chief to ask for help from the state authorities, to bring in marshals or detectives or whatever it took. Maybe, Klinger said, he should even ask for help from Allan Pinkerton and his men.

Given an opportunity to reply to the remarks of Mr. Klinger, Chief Farley was quoted as saying, "We don't need any help from no damned Pinkertons!" He later denied that he had said it.

Clint finished reading the newspapers just about the time he finished the last cup of coffee in the pot. He now knew just about all there was to know about these murders—at least, all that had been written in the newspapers.

He stood up, removed his jeans, and put on something more suitable for dinner in Denver. Reading about the Pinkertons reminded him of a couple of lady Pinkertons he'd known over the years. They were gone now, having moved on. There were really no women left in the city that he knew. He had a friend here, a detective named Talbot Roper who had once been a Pink himself until a falling-out with old Allan. He'd have to look Roper up.

Properly dressed in a black suit and white shirt, he put on his hat and then took the Colt New Line from his bag and tucked it into the waistband of his trousers, at the small of his back. Like most cities, Denver frowned on gun belts worn openly, but Clint was not the kind of man who could walk around without a gun. Once he had it firmly tucked behind his back, he was truly properly dressed and left the room to meet Bat Masterson for dinner.

SEVEN

Herbert George stared across his desk at his ace reporter and columnist Earl Klinger.

"What did Farley have to say for himself?" George asked.

"The same as always," Klinger said. He was tall, in his thirties, a gangly man no woman would ever call attractive. Many of his colleagues wondered, then, why the man did so well with the opposite sex. Maybe it was the power of his column that attracted them; Klinger was the premier crime columnist in Denver—despite what the *Denver Post* might have claimed. " 'An arrest is imminent.' "

"And is one?"

Klinger was sprawled in George's visitor's chair, his long legs straight out in front of him, crossed at the ankles.

"They're not even close."

"We need to find a new angle on this, Earl."

"Like what?"

"I met a man, today."

"Who?"

"His name is Clint Adams."

Klinger sat forward.

"The Gunsmith?"

"That's right."

"He's in Denver?"

George nodded.

"He's staying with Bat over at the Olympic."

Klinger snapped his fingers.

"That's right, they're old friends."

"I've been trying to get Bat interested in the murders, but he's so damned involved with his fights and his club."

"You want Bat to write about the murders? I thought *I* was the crime columnist on this paper."

"You are, Earl, but it could only increase our readership to have Bat take an interest. After all, he is Bat Masterson."

"He may be a legend as a gunman, a lawman, and a gambler, Herbert, but he's no writer."

"Tell that to the people who read his column."

This was a sore spot with Klinger. He had been writing for papers across the country, from Philadelphia to Los Angeles, learning his craft along the way. When Herbert George had offered him this job with *George's Weekly* he had jumped at it. He saw it as a stepping stone to the job he really wanted, writing for the *New York Morning Telegraph*. When these murders started to happen, he realized that this could be his big chance. If, however, Herbert George got Bat Masterson writing about them, that's what people would notice—not because Masterson was a better writer, but because he *was* Bat Masterson.

Klinger had been hearing that for months, ever since Masterson talked George into hiring him, and he was damned sick of it.

"Earl, Bat is no threat to you—"

"You bet he isn't," Klinger said, standing up. "And I'm going to prove it."

"Earl—"

But Klinger was already out the door, slamming it behind him.

As far as Herbert George was concerned, he needed both Klinger and Bat Masterson. They each pulled in a lot of readers, but if push came to shove and he had to back one of them . . . well, maybe it wouldn't come to that.

Earl Klinger had no doubt that if Herbert George were going to back one man he would choose Bat Masterson. After all, he *was* Bat Masterson. What he hoped to do, however, was come up with something that would make it impossible for Herbert George to let him go—at least before he was ready to go himself.

The only thing he could think of was to come up with the killer.

EIGHT

Once again Clint found Bat in the bar, this time surrounded by a group of men who seemed to be hanging on his every word. As he got closer he realized that Bat was regaling them with tales of his many exploits, some of which—no doubt—involved him.

"Ah, gentlemen, speak of the devil and here he is. This is my friend, Clint Adams."

Clint found himself shaking hands all around and not catching anyone's name.

"We have to go to dinner now, boys," Bat said. "Maybe you can talk to Clint later."

Bat took Clint's arm and led him away.

"Don't ever let them corner you," he said in almost a whisper, "they won't let you go without telling them a bunch of stories."

"And I will . . . about you."

Bat laughed.

"That'd be all right, then. Do you mind having dinner here, even though you already had lunch?"

"No, I don't mind. You were right, your cook is good."

"Good. Maybe tomorrow I'll take you around to some other places—but then, you've been to Denver many times before, haven't you, Clint?"

"I have."

"And you have friends here. What's his name? Talbot Roper?"

"That's right."

"I read about him in the papers from time to time."

"Have you ever written about him?"

"You forget, my area is sports. I stick to fighting and horse racing, occasionally some wrestling and even—if you can believe it—baseball. Hey, you played some baseball, didn't you?"

"Some in the East, a while back."

As they sat at the same table, in the same chairs, Bat said, "We could talk about that when I interview you."

Clint laughed.

"I don't remember agreeing to any interview, Bat."

"Well, Herbert isn't going to leave me alone until I get you to agree, and who would you rather have do it than me? Some snot-nosed kid reporter?"

"I'm not sure I want to have it done at all."

The waiter, Dave, came over and took their order. On Bat's recommendation Clint ordered the same thing he did, the beef stew.

"Did you get those newspapers I sent you?" Bat asked after Dave went to fill their order.

"I did, and I'm afraid I made a fool of myself in the process."

"Oh, this I got to hear."

Clint told Bat what he had thought when he opened the door and saw the blond woman in the hall, and then he told his friend what he'd said. Bat was laughing throughout the whole explanation, and Clint suddenly realized something.

"You planned that. You rat!"

Bat continued to laugh.

"You knew I'd think you sent her to me, didn't you?"

"I thought you might, yeah," Bat admitted, "and I thought it'd be pretty funny if you did. How did Del take it?"

"Not very well, as you might imagine. She got pretty insulted and called me names."

"I'm sorry," Bat said. "I'll square it with her, I swear. Um, what names did she call you?"

"Well . . . it wouldn't have been so bad if I hadn't lost my sheet."

"Oh, tell me about that."

"I will, if you'll try to contain yourself."

"I'll try."

But try as he might Bat couldn't keep from laughing, and soon tears were streaming from his eyes.

"Go on, laugh. It was all your doing, anyway."

"You have to admit, old friend, that it isn't often you make a fool of yourself with a woman."

"Well, I hope it will be a long time before it happens again."

"I told you, I'll straighten it out with her," Bat said.

"Who is she, anyway?"

"Del? Only the boss's niece."

"Herbert George's niece?"

Bat nodded.

"Her parents sent her here from the East to learn the newspaper business. She's been here two months and she knows more than I do already."

"And how hard can that be?" Clint asked.

"Just for that you can fish your own bacon out of the fire with her."

"What makes you think I'll ever see her again?"

"I didn't tell her who you were," Bat said. "When she finds out, you'll see her again. She's like everyone else in this town, looking for a story."

"Seems like you've got one going already."

"The murders?"

Clint nodded.

"I hope the police find this son of a bitch soon. As it is, I'm afraid to let my Emma walk the streets."

"How is Emma, Bat?"

"Oh, she's fine. She's pretty mad at me for all the time I'm putting in here, but . . . ah, she understands. She'd be glad for a chance to see you."

"If she's got the time that'd be fine."

Clint knew Bat was just being kind. Emma didn't like him much, he knew that. She put too much stock in his reputation, which was odd for a woman married to Bat Masterson.

Dinner came and they set about polishing it off.

"How about some poker tonight?" Bat asked when they were having coffee.

"If you need me for it."

"What do you mean? The game will be in your honor."

"Who'll be playing?"

"You, me, Quay, Herbert George—"

"If he comes back."

"He'll be back. He's still looking to get an interview out of you."

"Who else will be playing?"

"I don't know. We'll have to see. Maybe Earl Klinger."

"Klinger? I read some of his columns in the papers you gave me. He's very good."

"He's damned good, and he resents the hell out of me."

"Why's that?"

"Because he doesn't think I can write. He didn't approve when Herbert hired me to be a columnist. He's been a writer all his life. I guess he feels I don't belong on the same paper as him. He might be right, at that."

"I haven't read your columns, Bat, but Herbert George didn't strike me as the kind of man who would risk the credibility of his newspaper if he didn't think you were any good."

Bat waved the compliment away.

"It's my name he was after, but that's fine with me. I get to do what I want, write what I want, and I'm not shy about singing the praises of my own club. What do you say we see about that poker game?"

"Sounds good to me," Clint said, standing along with his friend. "Lead on."

NINE

The poker game took place in a private room in Bat's club, so since his arrival in Denver Clint still had not left the premises. So far that was all right with him, but tomorrow he wanted to get out and take a look at Denver. He hadn't seen it in some time, and he had always liked the city. Plus he wanted to get in touch with Talbot Roper again.

The room was not overly large. In fact, it was just big enough for the round table in the center and a small bar on one side with a bartender in place.

When Clint entered and saw that the room was permanently set up for poker, he turned and looked at Bat suspiciously.

"What?" Bat asked innocently.

"Am I being roped into a regular game, here?"

"I swear there's no regular game on Thursday nights, Clint."

Clint waited for the kicker and it soon came.

."The regular game is Friday night," Bat added. "You can play in that game, too, if you like, tomorrow night."

"Let's see how tonight's game goes," Clint said. "Are these all the same players?"

"Some of them are. Some of them were not available for an extra game, so we had to substitute. I'd say you'll be playing with about half the regular game."

At the moment Bat, Clint, and the bartender were the only ones in the room. The two friends walked over to the bar and each ordered a beer. Once he started playing, Clint would not drink at all. Bat usually nursed a beer along during a game.

"Who's playing?" Clint asked.

"Quay and probably Herbert George."

"And you, that makes three from the regular game. How many do you play?"

"Usually six or seven. Any more and we restrict the game to five-card stud."

"So, who else?"

"Farley might play."

"The chief of police?"

Bat nodded.

"He plays about half the time."

"How would he know about this game?"

"I sent a messenger."

"Do you really think he'll play, with what's happening with the women?"

"Oh, sure," Bat said. "He'll need to get his mind off all that stuff."

"Are they any good?"

Bat frowned and said, "Not in my league—or yours, for that matter."

Clint looked at his friend and said playfully, "Like my league and your league are so far apart?"

"You're okay."

"Thanks a lot."

The truth of the matter was Clint knew that Bat Masterson was a better card player than he was. In fact, Bat was probably better than most of the people he and Clint had ever played, with the possible exception of Luke Short.

As if reading his mind, Bat asked, "Have you heard anything from Luke Short lately?"

The conversation moved into those kinds of questions. Bat asked if Clint had talked to Wyatt Earp recently, Clint asked if Bat had seen or heard of Ben Thompson. They talked about mutual acquaintances like Buckskin Frank Leslie, Doc Holliday, and Bill Tilghman. Clint also asked about Bat's brother, Ed. Bat said he didn't know exactly what Ed was doing these days.

"He's moving around."

"He should settle down, like you."

"Not likely," Bat said.

At that moment the door opened and two men walked in. They were so deep in conversation that they did not miss a beat as they entered the room.

Clint knew one man, having met him earlier that afternoon—Herbert George, the publisher.

"The other man is Farley," Bat said.

"Doesn't he have a first name?" Clint asked.

"Yeah," Bat said, "Chief."

George and Farley were discussing the murders of the four women and what Farley was doing to apprehend the killer.

"I'm not gonna tell you what I'm doin', Herbert,

because you'll put it in your damn newspaper."

Farley was a big-bellied man wearing a rumpled three-piece suit. He had huge muttonchops that seemed to fan out from his plump cheeks. He was a tall man, as well, easily six two or three. "Massive" was the word that came to Clint's mind.

"If you two will stop discussing business," Bat called out, "I'll let you have a drink. Chief, I want to introduce you to a friend of mine."

"Clint Adams," Farley said. He studied Clint for a few seconds before finally extending his hand.

"Have we met?" Clint asked, accepting the proffered handshake. Farley's hand was big, but soft. It was also damp, like a kitchen dishcloth.

"No, but I recognize you, sir. That's my business."

"Beer, Chief?" Bat asked.

"Don't mind if I do."

As Farley stepped past Clint to the bar, Herbert George came up to him and asked, "Have you decided about that interview?"

"Not yet, Mr. George."

"Call me Herbert, please," the publisher said. "If I'm going to be taking your money we should be on a first name basis, don't you think?"

Clint was about to answer when the door opened and several men entered at one time. It seemed that the game would be starting fairly soon.

Without waiting for a reply, Herbert George moved to the bar.

Among the men who had entered Clint recognized only Frank Quay. The other two men were eventually introduced in turn.

First was a man named Judge E. T. Wells, and he was introduced as Bat's attorney. He was a man in his sixties who had apparently left the bench four years earlier to go into private practice.

The second man was Earl Klinger.

"I've read some of your columns," Clint said, shaking the man's hand.

"Really? Where would you have done that?"

"Here in Denver. After I heard about the murders I did some reading up on them. Even though the subject was gruesome, I enjoyed your columns."

"Well, thanks very much. I appreciate that."

Once everybody had a drink, they gathered around the table and sat down. There were seven men, so they decided they'd play seven-card stud. Bat supplied the fresh decks, and they played with cash instead of chips. It was a practice Clint enjoyed. He liked the way a pot looked in the center of the table with paper money.

"If nobody objects," Bat said, cracking a fresh deck, "I'll deal first."

Nobody objected, and the game got under way.

TEN

For the first hour, five of the seven players played even. Bat was winning big, and Earl Klinger was losing big. The stakes had started out fairly small, but a fifty- or hundred-dollar bet was no longer unusual. Clint had a feeling that the Friday night game was played for even higher stakes. He also had a feeling that of all the men in the room Earl Klinger was the one who could ill afford to lose this much money. There was something going on, though, between Klinger and Bat Masterson that no one else seemed a part of, or aware of. Klinger seemed intent on keeping Bat honest, even when everyone else in the room knew that he had a winning hand. It was clear that Klinger was no poker player.

Two hours into the game Klinger was sweating and still trying to keep Bat honest. The cards had begun to change, though, and the number of hands that Klinger could challenge Bat lessened, so while he was continuing to lose, he was not losing quite so heavily.

Suddenly, the cards started swinging from Bat to Clint to Frank Quay and back again. Herbert George had started to lose big, but he didn't seem concerned. Chief Farley played cards while puffing on a big cigar, and that seemed to satisfy him. He was rarely in a hand long enough to lose a large sum of money, and the pots he took were likewise small. For him playing and smoking seemed to be the thing.

Conversation was spare. On occasion Herbert George would ask Chief Farley something about the case of the murdered girls, but that was only between hands. Farley would either not answer or would brush the question off with a curt, "Not now."

Earl Klinger, for all his reputation as a tough newspaperman, never once brought up the subject. He seemed intent on watching Bat and catching him sooner or later in a big hand.

Clint knew it would never happen. Klinger knew no such thing, and as he continued to try he became agitated and frustrated.

"A break, gentlemen?" Bat asked after three hours.

No one argued.

They all rose from the table, and while some went to the small bar in the room, others left the room to stretch their legs and get some coffee.

"Coffee at this hour?" Clint said to Bat. It was well after midnight, and this was not Dodge City, where saloons stayed open until the last customer crawled out. "Where will they get it?"

"Downstairs," Bat said. "I keep someone in the kitchen and in the dining room most of the time when there's a game."

"Why not bring it into the room?"

"That wouldn't give some people an excuse to stretch their legs."

Clint looked around. Both Herbert George and Earl Klinger had left the room for coffee. The others were having beer.

Bat told Clint to remain at the table, and eventually the bartender came over with two beers.

"What's happening between you and Klinger?" Clint asked.

"It's the newspaper thing," Bat said. "Ever since I got hired to write a column, he's been trying to prove I don't belong."

"At this table it's he who doesn't belong," Clint said.

"That's painfully clear. He keeps trying to catch me bluffing."

"Keeping you honest is going to break him," Clint said.

"I'll take his marker," Bat said. "I've got a drawer full."

"Does he honor them?"

Bat nodded and said, "Most of the time . . . eventually."

"What about Farley?"

"He never loses more than he can afford."

"On his salary how does he even afford to play?"

Bat eyed Clint and said, "That's a naive question."

"He's taking money?"

Bat shrugged, and Clint realized that was a naive question, as well.

"How are you doing?" Bat asked.

"I'm ahead."

"So am I."

"Big surprise."

The one thing about playing with cash was that it was harder to tell who was winning and who was losing just by looking at the table. There were no stacks of chips in front of the players, and the money went in and out of their pockets as the game progressed.

"How much longer will we go?" Clint asked.

"My guess is Farley will drop out in about an hour. After that the rest of us will be able to breathe easier."

"I lost count," Clint said. "How many cigars has he gone through?"

"I don't know. He's never without one in his mouth. Herbert will quit soon after, as will Wells."

"And Klinger?"

"I'm afraid Earl will stay as long as we play."

Clint looked around the table.

"I think Quay's ahead," he said.

"He usually wins, but not much. He's too conservative, never takes a chance."

Clint had already figured out that when Quay stayed in it was usually because he had something. Judge Wells, on the other hand, seemed to rarely fold and took great delight in filling a straight, or a flush, even when he lost in the end to a full house.

Eventually, Klinger and George drifted back into the room. Klinger had a sour look on his face.

"Same story," Bat said. "Herbert tries to get Klinger to quit, but he just won't do it."

"Are they close?"

"They were once."

"Have they fallen out over you?"

"I'm afraid so, but what can I do about it? I love

writing that column. I ain't about to give it up."

"Then don't," Clint said. "Let them work their differences out between them."

"My sentiments exactly," Bat said. He stood up and called out, "Play is ready to resume, gentlemen. I suggest you retake your seats so that we can get under way."

They all came back to the table and sat down. Chief Farley lit up a fresh cigar and said, "I'm ready."

"I know your plan, Chief," Herbert George said. "You'll keep smoking those things until we all suffocate and then take off with the money."

The others laughed, except for Klinger. In fact, most of the men looked refreshed by the break, except for him. He was still sweating and looked even more disheveled than the chief.

"Cards are comin' out, gents," Bat said, starting to deal. "Good luck."

ELEVEN

Bat was right about Herbert George. He quit an hour into the second half of the game.

"I've got a paper to run in the morning," he said, rising. He looked at Clint and added, "It was a pleasure."

"I enjoyed it, too," Clint said.

"Of course you did," George said wryly. "You have a lot of my money in front of you."

Clint sat back in his chair, spread his arms wide, and said, "Better luck next time."

George looked at Earl Klinger and said, "What about you, Earl?"

Klinger looked down at his dwindling cash and said, "Are you kiddin'? I've got these guys right where I want 'em."

The publisher gave his reporter a long look, but Klinger ignored him and the man finally left, shaking his head.

The game went on for another hour, and Earl Klinger started drinking whiskey as the game progressed and he grew more frustrated. Chief Farley finally dropped out without getting hurt too badly. Clint thought that if Klinger had been sober he probably would have taken the opportunity to walk out with the man and question him about the murders. As it was, Farley just walked out with clouds of cigar smoke following him.

That left Clint, Bat, Frank Quay, Judge Wells—who had already lasted much longer than Bat expected—and Earl Klinger.

"It's gettin' late, boys," Bat said. "What do you say we set a time limit?"

"I think my time limit is up," Wells finally said. "If someone will point me to the door, I'll be leaving."

Wells shook hands with Clint and then took his leave.

"What do you say?" Bat asked again. "Time limit?"

"You afraid I'm gonna start winnin' my money back, Bat?" Earl Klinger asked.

"I ain't afraid of nothin', Earl," Bat said. "It's just gettin' late, that's all."

"What do you think, Quay?" Klinger asked. "Is it getting late for you?" He didn't wait for an answer, but turned to Clint and asked, "Or you?"

"It is getting kind of late, Mr. Klinger," Clint said. "I was on a train most of the day."

"I just need another hour, that's all," Klinger said, looking from Clint to Frank Quay and back. "Another hour to get my money back."

"You want your money back that bad, Earl," Bat said, "hell, I'll give it to you. How much did you lose?"

"I don't want you to *give* it back," Klinger said. "I want to win it back from you."

"Hell, Earl," Bat said, "everybody knows you ain't got much of a chance in hell of doin' that."

Klinger stood up and said, "So, everybody knows that, huh?"

"You're drunk, Earl," Bat said coldly, "or you wouldn't be lookin' at me like that."

"I'll show you how drunk I am," Klinger said. He picked up the rest of his money and said, "I got five hundred dollars here. I'll bet it on one hand, seven cards, dealt faceup."

Bat made a face.

"What kind of nonsense is that?" he asked.

"Sounds like a good idea to me," Clint said. "I'll play."

"So will I," Quay said.

"No," Klinger said, "just me and Bat."

"Hell, Earl," Quay said, "you don't even get even if you win with just the two of you. With me and Clint it's a two thousand-dollar pot."

"They got a point, Earl," Bat said. "With the four of us in, I'll play your game."

Klinger looked around the table and said, "All right, then."

"But you've got to sit down," Bat said.

Klinger hesitated, then sat.

"Whose deal is it?" Bat asked.

"The last deal was Farley's," Clint said, "that means you deal, Bat."

"No!" Klinger said.

"What?" Bat asked in disbelief.

"I—I don't want Bat to deal."

"It's his deal, Earl," Quay said.

"I want Clint to deal."

"Earl—" Quay said.

"Deal 'em, then," Bat said, interrupting him. "I want this game to end before tomorrow night's starts."

Clint shuffled the cards and then started to deal seven-card stud, but all seven cards up. He dealt first to Klinger, then Quay, then Bat, and then himself.

Seven of diamonds to Klinger.

Three of clubs to Quay.

Bat got a jack of hearts.

Clint dealt himself a four of spades.

Second time around.

"Eight of clubs to Earl, possible straight . . .

"King of spades for Frank . . .

"Ace of clubs to Bat . . .

"Dealer gets a jack of diamonds. Bat is high."

Third card.

Klinger got a ten of spades. He now had seven, eight, ten toward a straight.

Quay got a two of spades. He had a king of spades to go with it and the three of clubs.

Bat received a seven of clubs, giving him two clubs—ace, seven—and a jack of hearts.

Clint got a ten of hearts to go with his diamond jack and the four of spades.

Fourth card.

"Three of hearts to Earl, that sort of busts his straight."

"There's time," Klinger said, rubbing his hands while he watched the cards fall.

"Five of spades to Frank, showing three spades now, and also a two, three, five toward a straight."

"So he's got three cards to a small straight," Klinger said. "I got three cards to a bigger one."

"Bat gets a five of diamonds, no help."

Clint dealt himself another jack, giving him a pair.

"Two jacks looking good," Quay said.

"There's still three more cards," Klinger announced.

Clint dealt out the fifth card.

"Pair of eights for Earl," he said, as he dropped an eight of hearts on the man.

"Ha!" Klinger said, slapping his hands together once and wetting his lips.

"Ace of diamonds to Frank," Clint said. "Needs a four for a straight.

"Bat gets queen of spades, and the dealer a two of clubs, no help."

Sixth card.

"A six of spades for Earl, he needs a nine for a straight."

"Yes!" Klinger said.

"Frank gets a jack, no real help there . . .

"Nine of diamonds for Bat, doesn't look good . . .

"I get a queen, no help there. My jacks are still high."

"I've got eights, and I need a nine for a straight," Klinger said.

"We can see it, Earl," Quay said.

Bat, quiet the whole time, was not about to speak before the last card was dealt.

Seventh, and last card.

"Nine for Earl, he's got his straight."

"Whoo-ee!" Klinger shouted.

"Pair of three for Quay . . .

"Six of diamonds for Bat, no help . . .

"An eight of spades for me." Clint put the card

down and said, "Earl wins."

"Goddamn!" Klinger shouted. He stood up and raked the money in.

"Good hand, Earl," Bat said.

"You're damn right it's a good hand, a winning hand!" Klinger said happily, his eyes glazed with his good fortune and with liquor.

"I'm glad you won, Earl," Bat said.

"Huh?" Klinger said, squinting across the table at Bat.

"I truly am . . . but don't ever come back here."

"What?"

"You heard me," Bat said. "You insulted me by not wanting me to deal, even after I agreed to play your stupid game. Take your money and make it last. You don't play poker here anymore. In fact, you're not welcome in my club anymore."

"That's bein' a sore loser," Klinger said.

"You've been a sore loser all night, Earl, and nobody said a word," Quay said. "Then Bat gave you a chance to get even."

"And I did, by God!"

"Be happy with it, then. I think you better leave."

Klinger looked across the table at Bat.

"This is because I'm a better writer than you, isn't it? Because I have a better column."

"You are a better writer than me, Earl," Bat said. "Nobody ever questioned that . . . but I do question that your column is more interesting than mine."

"How can you—" Klinger started, but Bat stood up so quickly that he knocked his chair over behind him. Klinger stopped short and just stared.

"Time to go, Earl," Bat said.

Klinger finished picking his money up from the table and stuffing it in his pockets, never taking his eyes off Bat.

"I ain't afraid of you, Bat Masterson," he said, backing toward the door. "And I'll tell you another thing, nobody will question whose column is better when I expose the killer of these women . . . nobody!"

With that he opened the door, went out, and slammed the door behind him.

"You think he really knows who the killer is?" Quay asked.

"It's the liquor talking," Bat said.

Quay looked around and then announced unnecessarily, "Game's over, I guess."

"It's over," Bat said. He picked up his money and, despite having just lost five hundred dollars, he was still ahead. Clint was about a hundred dollars up, while Quay had broken just about even.

"See you fellas tomorrow," Quay said, starting for the door. Before he reached it, though, he turned and said, "Can I ask you something?"

"Go ahead," Clint said.

"You didn't let him win, did you?"

"If you let somebody win," Bat said, "it ain't gambling, and it ain't poker."

Quay thought about that, then nodded and went out.

Bat looked at Clint and asked, "You didn't let him win, did you?"

TWELVE

The killer was angry.

He wasn't angry at the woman, but it was the woman who would be the target of his anger. Too bad for her, but it never occurred to the killer to try his hand at killing a man.

He went down to the square that was known for its prostitutes. It was late and most of the street whores were inside with their last customers of the night. There were usually some stragglers, though, and that was what the killer was looking for.

He found one.

She was a little bit of a thing with a shawl wrapped around her shoulders. Katy Miller knew she was not a beauty. She also knew that keeping her shawl as tightly around her shoulders as she did would not add to her already dwindling appeal. And any appeal that she had faded even more when some of the other girls were around. It was only when she was alone that Katy attracted customers, and then only the ones other girls had turned away.

Katy Miller was forty-eight and her best years as a whore were behind her . . . that is, if a whore can have years that can be called her "best." The only reason she could keep working at her age was because of her size. Being as small as she was made her look younger.

She was starting to doubt that she'd even find a customer for the end of the night when she saw the man crossing the street toward her.

"It's cold," he said.

Trying to appear coy she asked, "What did you have in mind?"

"You should be warm."

"I can make you warm, darlin'," she said, moving closer to him. It was only when she pressed up against him that she felt the tip of the blade.

"Blood is very warm," he said in her ear just before thrusting the blade into her belly and slitting her wide open while holding his hand over her mouth. From across the street anyone would think they were simply locked in an embrace.

And as far as the killer was concerned, they were.

It was funny but all Katy Miller could think was that he was right. Her blood *did* feel warm as it poured down over her belly and legs. . . .

THIRTEEN

Before turning in for the night—or morning—Bat asked Clint to meet him for breakfast.

"Okay, but what do you say we eat somewhere else for a change?"

Bat laughed.

"Okay. Meet me in the lobby at nine and I'll take you to a nice place for breakfast. It's right near here."

"Make it nine-thirty and it's a deal."

"Done."

Bat accompanied Clint upstairs and showed him where his own room was, at the end of the hall. It was where he stayed when it was too late for him to go home to Emma.

"I'd show you the inside, but it's a mess."

"What, no maids?"

"This ain't a hotel. That reminds me, keep your room clean yourself because there *is* no maid."

"I'll remember."

52

They stopped at Clint's room for a moment.

"This thing between you and Klinger . . ."

"It was never as bad as tonight, but he was losing, and drinking, and I don't think he and Herbert were getting along too well."

"Are you making excuses for him?"

"No," Bat said, "not for what he did to me, anyway. He showed disrespect to me in my own place. I'll stick to my guns, Clint. I don't want him back here."

"That's your decision, Bat, but what do you think about what he said there at the end?"

"About the killer?"

Clint nodded.

"Just liquor talk," Bat said. "If he knew who the killer was, he would have exposed him by now and written about it. He'd be on his way to New York. No, I don't think he knows who it is."

"Maybe he's going to try to find out."

"That's the job of the police."

"I guess so."

"Why, you want to deal yourself a hand in that game? Don't you let yourself get drawn into enough trouble without going to look for it yourself?"

"No, no, I don't want to get involved," Clint said. "It's just a shame, that's all."

"It's a shame that the victims are just whores."

"What do you mean?"

"I mean if they were respectable women this city would be up in arms. The mayor would be all over Farley, and he'd be getting something done."

"You don't think Farley's doing his job?"

"All I know is if somebody like, oh, Bill Tilghman was chief of police there'd be more getting done."

"Well, Bill's sort of a special case," Clint said. "He

really thinks he was born to uphold the law."

"Okay, then, if Wyatt was chief you think he'd be sitting on his butt playing poker?"

"No."

"There, see—"

"Faro, maybe," Clint added, "but not poker."

"Ah, never mind," Bat said. "I'm going to sleep. I'll see you in the morning."

"Good night," Clint said, and went into his room.

He had to remove some of the newspapers from the bed so he could pull the bed covers down. As he did he paused to look at some of them again. Obviously, Bat was speaking from much more knowledge than he had, but he was surprised if the city of Denver was not at least concerned about these murders. Hell, they should be downright horrified. Who was to say that the killer would not suddenly start picking women arbitrarily, instead of sticking with whores?

Was it possible that this kind of killing spree could be going on and the chief of police was not doing all he could to stop it?

Clint decided that his friend Talbot Roper would have some serious opinions about this. After breakfast tomorrow he'd go and talk to him about it . . . just out of curiosity.

FOURTEEN

In the morning Clint found a somber-looking Bat Masterson waiting for him in the lobby. He had a newspaper in his hand.

"Regretting your decision to ban Klinger from your club?"

"Take a look at this," Bat said, handing Clint the paper.

It was a copy of *George's Weekly* and the headline proclaimed: FIFTH VICTIM STABBED, MUTILATED.

"Jesus," Clint said, "another one?"

"Don't bother reading the story," Bat said. "It's just like the others. He got her on the street, pulled her into an alley, and mutilated her."

Clint shook his head and handed back the paper.

"He's getting more brazen," Bat said. "They said there was a lot of blood right on the sidewalk. He stabbed her right out where anyone could have seen him."

"And yet no one did?"

"No one who's talking, anyway."

"You're a little more upset about this than you were last night."

"This has Emma scared out of her wits, Clint. This is our city. I mean, we've chosen to live here and look what's happening."

"Why do I get the feeling you're talking yourself into doing something?"

"Jesus, this woman was forty-eight years old! She paid her dues working the streets a long time ago, she didn't deserve to be killed like this. But you know what? There are people in this town who will say she did."

"Bat—"

"Come on, I promised you some breakfast. We can talk about this on the way."

Their destination turned out to be only two blocks away, a small café where the owner, a pale, soft-looking man in his fifties, seemed to know Bat and showed him right to a table against the wall.

"Bring us a couple of special breakfasts, Billy," Bat said.

"Comin' right up, Bat."

"So you do eat someplace other than your own club sometimes."

"Sometimes," Bat said, "especially when I want to eat alone."

Bat put the newspaper on the table and kept his hand on it.

"Bat, tell me what you think you can do?"

"I can make some inquiries," his friend said right away. "I can talk to Farley and see what he's got."

"If you want to do something, why don't you hire the Pinkertons?"

"Ha! The day I can't do a better job than old Allan Pinkerton . . ." He didn't bother finishing the sentence.

Clint had had his own run-ins with Allan Pinkerton over the years and knew that the man was not easy to get along with. He did, however, respect the man's abilities.

"Well, if you don't want to talk to Pinkerton, how about my friend, Talbot Roper?"

Bat looked up from the table at Clint and said, "Now there's an idea. Roper's good, isn't he?"

"He's damn good, Bat. In fact, to tell you the truth, I was thinking about going to see him myself right after breakfast."

"Would you mind if I tagged along? I'd like to hear what he has to say about all of this."

"No problem. He's a busy man, though, travels a lot. I just hope he's in town."

"Let's go and find out," Bat said enthusiastically. He looked as if he was going to jump up from his seat right there and then.

"After breakfast," Clint said, "remember?"

"Oh, yeah," Bat said, settling back in his chair.

FIFTEEN

Bat went through his breakfast in half the time it took Clint and sat fidgeting and staring at the newspaper while Clint finished his.

"Okay," Clint said, even though he would have liked to have had more coffee. "Let's go."

Bat got to his feet and dropped money onto the table.

"That'll cover the check."

They stepped out into the street and Bat flagged down a cab.

"Give him Roper's address," Bat said as they got into the cab.

Clint did so and settled into his seat opposite his friend.

"I think you're getting yourself all worked up, Bat," he said.

"You think so?"

"Yes."

"So do I. Emma came by the club this morning and she was scared. She gave me the newspaper."

Clint had actually met Emma only once, when she and Bat went to a prizefight that Clint had also attended. Bat had met her here in Denver and married her recently. She had disapproved of Clint on the spot. She had also sworn that she would never attend another prizefight. Clint thought that secretly pleased Bat.

"You want to know what she said?"

"What?"

"She wondered if I couldn't get you to do something."

"Me? She doesn't even like me. Why would she want me to do something?"

"Because she'd rather not have me killed while I'm trying to do something."

"I see. She wants you to stay out of it and try to get me involved, so that if the killer kills me she won't feel so bad."

"She doesn't *dislike* you, Clint," Bat said diplomatically. "She just . . ."

"Doesn't like me. Look, Bat, I only intended to talk to Roper. I don't think you should think about hiring him—not with your own money anyway."

"That's a good idea," Bat said.

"What is?" Clint didn't know what good idea he had just come up with.

"I can get a citizens' committee to come up with a fund to hire Roper."

"If he wants to get involved."

"Are you kidding? He gets his name in the paper every chance he gets, and this would be a big chance."

"Well . . ." Clint said, starting to regret he'd ever mentioned Roper. "Maybe he'll be out of town." He was actually hoping that Roper would be out of town.

"I hope he's not," Bat said. "I want to meet this Roper, Clint. Hey, any friend of yours is a friend of mine, right?"

Clint wished that was the only reason. He had his own curiosity about what type of madman enjoyed mutilating women, but he'd never really intended to get personally involved . . . not really. Now he could feel himself getting sucked in by Bat's indignation and enthusiasm.

"We'll see. . . ."

As the cab pulled up in front of Talbot Roper's office, Bat almost climbed over Clint in his eagerness to get out. He didn't even make any attempt to pay for the cab and showed impatience when Clint did.

They approached Roper's door, which gave right out onto the street rather than being inside the building. The lettering on the door said: TALBOT ROPER, PRIVATE INVESTIGATIONS. Clint knocked and the door was answered by a woman he didn't know. Apparently Roper had changed secretaries again.

This one was tall and slender, with high, small breasts and black hair. Her skin was very pale, and her neck long. Her hair was piled on top of her head, but a few ringlets had fallen loose.

"Can I help you?"

"We'd like to see Mr. Roper," Bat said.

"Do you have an appointment?"

"No, but he's a friend of his," Bat said, not giving Clint a chance to speak, "and I'm Bat Masterson."

The woman looked at Bat for a moment without expression, then turned her attention to Clint. She was apparently unimpressed . . . so far.

"And you are?" she asked.

"Clint Adams."

"Oh, Mr. Adams." Now she was impressed. "Yes, Mr. Roper had told me about you. Please, come in."

"Is Tal here?" Clint asked as he eased past her, followed by Bat.

"Yes, he is."

As they entered, Clint saw that the office was in a state of disarray. Her desk was piled high with files, and there were others on the floor and on a chair.

"We're reorganizing the office, as you can see. Please wait a moment and I'll tell him you're here."

"Thank you."

She left them in her office and went into Roper's. Moments later he reappeared with her. He was a tall, handsome man in his forties, and Clint noticed some gray in his previously dark full head of hair.

"Clint, goddamn it, why didn't you let me know you were coming?"

"Hello, Tal."

The two men shook hands warmly.

"And this must be the famous Bat Masterson? I understand you're a Denver resident now."

"That's right." The two men shook hands. "Maybe you've read my column in *George's Weekly*? The sports page?"

"I'm afraid not," Roper said. "I'm afraid I'm a *Post* man myself."

"Oh."

Clint could see that Roper's remark deflated Bat

somewhat, and he stepped in before the moment could become awkward.

"You should give the *Weekly* a try, Tal. Bat knows what he's talking about."

"I don't doubt that he does. I heard you have a sports club now, Mr. Masterson?"

"That's right, down on Sixteenth and Market. We have a big fight coming in next week. I could leave a ticket for you."

Roper cast a quick look Clint's way, caught Clint's nod, and said, "That would be very nice. Thank you."

"Could we take up some of your time, Tal? We want to talk about something."

"Sure, if you don't mind the mess. Come into my office. Dolores? Coffee?"

"Coming up, boss."

"Let's go," Roper said. "I'm curious about what it is brings both of you here."

"I'm afraid it's murder, Tal," Clint said.

"Well, then, I guess we had better talk, hadn't we?"

SIXTEEN

"What's this about murder?" Roper asked from behind his desk.

They may have been rearranging the office, but Roper's was spotless. It was more precise to say they were rearranging the outer office.

"The prostitutes who are being murdered is what we're here to talk about. There was another one found this morning."

"I know that," Roper said. "What's your interest?"

"Me, I'm curious," Clint said, "but Bat lives here now and it bothers him that women are being killed on the streets."

Roper looked at Bat and said, "Too bad the chief of police doesn't have the same opinion."

"I didn't think Farley was trying very hard," Bat said.

"And he won't," Roper said, "not while the women who are being killed are just whores."

63

"What do you think of all this, Tal?" Clint asked.

"I think there's a crazy man out there cutting up women," Roper said. "Five that we know of, but who's to say how many he's actually killed."

"Something has to be done," Bat said.

"By whom?" Roper asked.

"Well, I was thinking of trying to do something, but I'm no detective."

"What about the Pinkertons?"

Bat made a disgusted sound.

"Who's doing the hiring here, Mr. Masterson?"

"Call me Bat."

"All right, Bat. What I mean is, who's putting up the money?"

"I'm going to get a group together to do that."

"And you'll want to hire me, then?"

"That's right."

"To do what?"

"To catch the bastard."

Roper thought for a moment.

"I'm one man, Bat," he said finally. "The police have a better chance of catching him."

"If they were interested, you mean."

"Yes," Roper said. "If they'd put some men on the street in disguise they'd probably end up catching this maniac."

"Is that what you'd do?" Clint asked. "Go into the street in disguise?"

Roper looked at Clint, then back at Bat.

"If I take this case I won't be discussing my methods with anyone," Roper said. "I never do."

"I don't care how you do it, as long as you get it done," Bat said.

"That's just it, Bat," Roper said. "I might not get it

done, but whether I do or not, I'll be putting in time and I'll have to be paid for that time. Understand? I don't get paid for results, I get paid for the time I put into a case."

Bat hesitated, then said, "All right, but you'll want to get results."

"Oh, yes," Roper said. "I'll want results, all right. I'll want this maniac off the streets more than anyone in town."

"But that will be because you're being paid?" Bat asked.

"That's right," Roper said. "It sounds mercenary, I know, but that's how I make my living. If that's acceptable to you, then I'll take the job."

"It's acceptable," Bat said.

"Normally I'd ask for a retainer," Roper said, "but since you're a friend of Clint's I'm willing to wait until you get your group together."

"Will you start immediately, though?"

"Oh, yes," Roper said, "but when you get your people together, and your funds, I'll want you to come back here and give Dolores a retainer."

As if on cue Dolores entered with a tray bearing a pot of coffee and three cups. The men suspended their conversation until she had poured and gone.

"Is that agreeable?" Roper asked, without missing a beat.

"Yes," Bat said.

Roper looked at Clint.

"What about you?"

"What about me?"

"What's your part in this?"

"I brought you two together."

"That's it?"

"Yes," Clint said. "Why are you asking?"

"Because I know you, Clint," Roper said. "I know you like to get involved in other people's problems. Well, here you've got an entire city's problem."

"I seem to remember the last time I was here I got involved in a problem of yours."

"I was in the hospital and I appreciated your help. What I want to know is, are you going to try and help me again?"

"Not if you don't need it."

"I'll hold you to that," Roper said.

The detective walked them back to the front door.

"Bat, I appreciate the offer of the tickets for the fight, but if I haven't caught the killer by then I won't be using them."

"I understand," Bat said.

Roper extended his hand and Bat took it.

"It's been a pleasure meeting you, sir. I've read and heard a lot about you."

"Only half of it is true," Bat said, "unfortunately, it's the bad half."

Roper laughed and said, "You mean there was a good half?"

SEVENTEEN

After Clint and Roper said good-bye, he and Bat stepped out into the street, Roper closing the door quietly but firmly behind them.

"This is going to be on your head," Bat said, pointing at Clint.

"What is?"

"If he doesn't come up with results."

"He explained that—"

"Look, when you hire somebody to do a job you let them do it on their terms," Bat said, "even when you don't like the terms."

"You didn't like his—"

"He gets paid whether he gets results or not? Who could like those terms?"

They started walking, keeping their eyes out for a cab.

"What are you going to tell your group?" Clint asked.

"I'm not going to tell them that, that's for sure. I'll just leave that part out."

"Tell me something, Bat."

"What?"

"What will you do if you can't get a group up?" Clint asked. "Foot the bill yourself?"

"Bite your tongue!"

"Then what?"

"I'll get a group up."

"But if not?"

"There's always Herbert."

"You think the *Weekly* will put up the money?"

"Maybe."

They walked a little further before Bat said, "And then there's you."

"I was waiting for that," Clint said.

"Well, you want him caught, too, don't you?"

"Sure, but what happened to that talk about keeping our friendship apart from business?"

"This would not be a business proposition."

"I'll be putting up money," Clint said, "you'll be putting up money, gee, that sure sounds like a business proposition to me."

"Well, it's not. It's just two concerned citizens pooling their resources—"

"You forget," Clint said. "I'm not a citizen."

"It was a figure of speech," Bat said. "You're here, ain't you? It's happening, you're interested, it's only natural you'd help . . . and not only with money."

"What the hell does that mean?"

"Well, you don't think I'm going to let Roper have all the fun, do you?"

Bat saw a cab and prepared to flag it.

"I promised Roper I wouldn't get involved."

"I didn't," Bat said, and stepped into the street to flag the cab down.

EIGHTEEN

After Clint Adams and Bat Masterson left the office, Talbot Roper talked with Dolores.

"I'll be gone for a while, Dolores."

"For how long?" she asked.

"As long as it takes."

"And what have we been hired to do, Mr. Roper?" she asked.

"You, my sweet, have been hired to run this office and not ask questions. So far, for the past couple of months, you've been doing a perfect job."

"Did you talk to all your assistants that way, Mr. Roper?"

"What way is that, Dolores?"

"That . . . familiar way."

"Well, I don't know," he said. "I talked to all my secretaries that way, but I don't think I've ever had an assistant before."

"I assume you'll be keeping in touch with me during your absence."

"Dolores, I think you'd better come into my office so we can go over this very carefully. . . . "

In the cab they continued to talk about the prostitute murders.

"What about Farley?" Clint asked.

"What about him?"

"What's going to happen when he finds out you've hired Roper?"

"Who says he's gonna find out?"

"One, you're going to get a group of people together. Somebody's going to talk. Two, the man probably has a lot of ears he keeps to the ground. You better figure out a story for when he does find out."

"Okay, I'll be able to take care of that. Farley is not a problem."

"What about George?"

"What about him?"

"You haven't thought this through, Bat," Clint said.

"What's to think about? I'm a citizen, I'm entitled to take steps to protect my home, my city."

"You're also a writer for George's paper. What you do reflects on him."

Bat thought a moment, then said, "That's not a problem."

"Why not?"

"I'll recruit him into the group."

"Him, or the paper?"

"Maybe both."

"And then there's Earl Klinger."

"What are you, the devil's advocate here?" Bat made a face and said, "Okay, what about Klinger?"

"If he finds out what you did, he's going to write

about it, and he's not going to put you in a good light."

"What could he say bad about me?"

"He'll think of something."

"Is there anyone else I should be thinking about?" Bat asked.

"One more, I guess."

"I was kidd—who?"

"Who's your biggest detractor in Denver?"

Bat stared at Clint and asked, "Floto?"

"You tell me."

"What could Otto do?"

"I don't know. I don't know what any of these people could do, Bat. I'm just saying you might be giving them some ammunition to play with. Think it over."

"Answer me a question now," Bat said.

"What?"

"If you're always asking so many questions," Bat said, "how do you manage to get into so much trouble?"

"That's easy," Clint said. "I'm a natural."

NINETEEN

When they returned to the club they agreed to
have lunch separately. Bat said he had some
"damned paperwork" to catch up on, and he'd probably just eat in his office.

"When you and Wyatt and I were out on the plains
hunting buffalo years ago, Bat," Clint said, "I never
thought I'd ever hear you say that you had an office."

"Neither did I," Bat said. "You have the run of the
place, Clint. Make yourself at home."

Bat waved and went to his office. Clint looked
around the Olympic Club and had no idea how to
make himself "at home" in such a place.

Earl Klinger had a hell of a hangover, and the
sneaking suspicion that he had made a fool out of
himself the night before.

"Earl!" Herbert George yelled from his office.

Klinger, who had himself only just arrived, responded by entering the office.

"Close the door," George said.

Klinger obeyed.

"What the hell was that all about, last night?" George demanded.

"I'm sure I'd have an answer for you, Herbert, if I knew what you were talking about."

"You know damn well what I'm talking about," George said. "The poker game last night."

"Oh, Jesus," Klinger said, "did I play poker last night?"

"You did."

"Good," Klinger said, putting his hands in his pockets and pulling out wads of money. He kept doing so until it was all on George's desk.

"What the hell is that?" George demanded.

"Apparently, I won last night."

George stared at the money on his desk.

"How much is there?"

"Two thousand dollars."

"Two thousand—when I left you barely had five hundred dollars in front of you."

"I know—at least, I think I know."

"You beat Quay, Clint Adams, *and* Bat Masterson at the poker table?"

"Apparently . . . but I think in the process I got banned from the club."

"For what?"

Klinger frowned.

"Near as I can remember, I think I accused Bat of cheating."

"Jesus! You're lucky you only got banned! He could have killed you."

"I guess so."

"Put your damn money away and sit down."

Klinger tucked the money back into his pockets and sat down.

"If you want to go after Bat Masterson, Earl, then do it on your terms, not his."

"What do you mean?"

"I mean in print, man, not at the poker table."

"But I won."

"I don't know how that happened—"

"Maybe I'm a good poker player."

"You're a terrible poker player, Earl!" Herbert George said. "You must have had one hell of a lucky streak last night. Believe me, I intend to ask Bat about it."

"Good," Klinger said, "when you find out what happened you can let me know."

"Earl, I know you've got a burr up your ass about Bat and his column, but don't make me have to choose between you."

"I think we had this conversation yesterday, Herbert," Klinger said testily. "You think Masterson's column can sell more papers for you than mine."

"I think both of you sell a hell of a lot of newspapers for me, Earl, and I'd like to keep it that way. But if you're intent on taking Bat on, then do it where you're at your best."

Klinger stood up.

"That's just a piece of advice," George added.

"I'll keep it in mind, Herbert," Klinger said, and left the office.

Frank Quay rose late that morning, understandably so since the poker game had gone on quite late last night. Not so late, though, that he hadn't been able to find himself a woman for the night.

Lying next to him, sound asleep and snoring, was a redhead. He wasn't sure where he'd found her, because when they got back to his room they had opened a bottle of whiskey. He did, however, remember that she had an odd and particular liking for having her belly button licked. He, himself, had a liking for licking her a little lower than that.

She was lying on her back, her big breasts flattened against her chest. Quay also had a liking for a particular kind of woman. He liked women who had large breasts and firm, round butts, but were skinny. This one had very large breasts, with dark brown nipples. Her butt could have been bigger, but he didn't hold that against her, not with breasts like that.

The sheet was covering her flat belly, and he folded it down to reveal her puckered navel. He leaned over and gently tickled her with his tongue until she began to squirm and reached for him. He could smell that she was suddenly ready and traced a wet path from her navel down to the tangled red bush between her legs. When he inserted his tongue there she whispered, "Oh yeah, luv," and took his head in her hands to keep him right there. . . .

When Quay dressed he paid the woman and saw her to the door.

"Again tonight, luv?" she asked.

In the light of day, now that they were out of bed, he could see that she wasn't really very pretty, and that was another thing he liked, girls with pretty faces. This one had managed to slip past him last night, and indeed she wasn't bad. He might very well seek her out some night if he couldn't find something better, but he wasn't about to make any promises.

"Why don't we wait and see what happens?" he asked.

"Well, you know my name if you want me. Ta."

That was the other thing that bothered him. She had a slight English accent and used words like "ta." He had no idea what that meant.

He patted her on the butt, gently pushing her out the door at the same time and lied, "That's right, I know your name."

TWENTY

Clint was sitting in the lobby of the Olympic Club, reading a newspaper and wondering what to do with his time when Del Perkins came walking in the door. Clint looked around for Bat, who was supposed to clear things up for him with the young woman, but his friend was nowhere in sight. He was going to have to do it himself.

He left the newspaper on the sofa and walked across the lobby toward her.

"Miss Perkins?"

She turned to see who had called out her name, and when she saw him her jaw firmed. He noticed that her eyes were a pretty green.

"You! What do you want, you pervert?"

He held up his hands in a placating gesture and said, "I only want to talk to you. I want to explain about what happened yesterday."

"What is there to explain? Look, I came here to

78

see Bat Masterson. He's supposed to introduce me to a friend of his. Have you seen him?"

"The friend?"

"No, Bat Masterson. Have you seen him?"

"Not since he and I had breakfast."

She turned to face him and said, "You had breakfast with him?"

"I did."

She frowned and asked, "Why am I getting a funny feeling about you?"

"What kind of feeling is that, Miss Perkins?"

"The feeling that you're Clint Adams."

"That's because I am."

"Oh, great."

"I assume I'm the friend Bat was supposed to introduce you to?"

"I'm afraid so."

"Good, that means we've already taken care of the introductions."

"Not exactly," she said. "I'm Delilah Perkins, Mr. Adams, from *George's Weekly*. I understand we're supposed to do an interview."

Now Clint frowned. He had the distinct feeling that he had been set up from the moment he arrived.

"We're having an interview if you're the one being interviewed," he said.

"I beg your pardon?"

"Somebody's been playing us both, Miss Perkins."

"Playing us? I don't understand."

"Our meeting yesterday was engineered."

"Look," she said impatiently, "all I know is that my uncle told me to come here and interview you. Are you backing out now?"

"I'm not backing out because I never agreed."

"I don't understand this. He told me that you had agreed to be interviewed. I'm getting the feeling somebody lied."

"You're a very astute young lady, aren't you?" Clint asked.

"There's no need for your sarcasm, Mr. Adams. If, as you say, we are both being played, I, for one, don't like it."

"Well, neither do I, Miss Perkins," he said. "Maybe we can have a cup of coffee and plot our revenge?"

She studied him for a moment and then said, "I'm still not convinced you're not a pervert."

"All I'm asking for is a chance to change your mind," he said. "What do you say?"

"What the hell," she answered with a shrug, "I'll take a chance."

TWENTY-ONE

It was too late for breakfast and too early for lunch so Clint and Delilah Perkins went into the club dining room to have coffee and pie. Since it was not a meal-time there were plenty of tables to be had, and Clint chose one in the back.

"I hope this is all right," Del said as they sat down. "I'm not a member."

"I am," Clint said, "at least, I think I am. Bat told me to make myself at home, so that's what I'm doing. You're my guest."

She squinted at him and said, "Before I find myself starting to like you, would you care to explain what happened yesterday?"

"All right," Clint said, "but you have to listen to the whole thing without interrupting before you make your judgment. Agreed?"

"Agreed."

They were served their coffee and pie and then he

explained what had happened, how he'd been awak-
ened and not expecting a woman at the door had
simply wrapped himself in the sheet. When he got to
the part about dropping the sheet and the newspapers, she actually started to laugh. He hoped this
meant that he was about to be forgiven, and maybe
even liked.

"That's it," he said, "that's my story. Do you still
think I'm a pervert?"

"No, I don't," she said, smiling. "I was too harsh
with you, Clint. I apologize."

"There's no apology necessary," Clint said. "It's
enough that you've changed your opinion of me.
Thank you."

"You're welcome," she said. "Now let's talk about
the interview."

He hesitated a moment, then said, "You're
sneaky."

"Look, whether we like it or not, I've been as-
signed to interview you."

"Get yourself another assignment."

"Why won't you give us an interview?"

"I've given interviews before, Del—do I have to
call you that?"

"My real name is Delilah."

"That's a beautiful name. Why would you shorten
it?"

"My father wanted a boy. My mother called me
Delilah, but my father called me Del."

"Can I call you Delilah, then?"

"Sure," she said, "why not?"

"Delilah, I've done my share of interviews in the
past and none of them have come out very well."

"Then you need one to be done right."

"Maybe so, but—"

"I think you're weakening," she said, sliding her chair back.

"Where are you going?"

"I have other work to do."

"You've finished trying to talk me into an interview?" he asked.

"No," she said, "I've just finished for now."

He stood up.

"How about dinner tonight?"

"Can we talk about the interview then?"

"Sure," he said, "I guess there's no harm in talking about it."

She smiled.

"You're weakening."

"We'll see."

She put her hand out impulsively and he took it.

"I'm glad we had a chance to talk, anyway."

"I wasn't going to leave Denver without clearing things up."

"Well, now that we have cleared things up, I hope you won't be leaving too soon."

"No," he said, "not too soon."

"Then I'll see you tonight. I'll meet you here. Is that all right?"

"That's fine, Delilah."

"See you later, Clint."

It was then they both realized that he hadn't released her hand yet.

"I'll walk you to the lobby," he said, letting her hand go.

They walked to the lobby together and said goodbye again there. He watched her walk out, then detected a presence behind him.

"Guess you didn't need me to introduce the two of you, huh?" Bat asked.

"You son of a bitch!"

"What?"

"Did you tell George to have her work on me about the interview?"

"That was a good idea," Bat said, "but I think Herbert came up with it on his own. Did you do the interview?"

"No."

"Are you gonna do it?"

"No."

"Are you gonna see her again?"

"Tonight, for dinner."

"Well," Bat said, smiling, "I guess she doesn't think you're a pervert anymore."

"No thanks to you," Clint said.

TWENTY-TWO

Herbert George looked up angrily as his office door opened, but when he saw it was his niece, Del, the anger faded.

"I thought for a moment you were Earl Klinger," George said to her. "He's trying my patience."

"And you're trying mine, Uncle Herbert."

George sat back in his chair and regarded his niece. Since the death of her father last year, Delilah had not been getting along with her mother, George's younger sister. They didn't live together, Del was too old for that, but they had reacted to her father's death differently. While Delilah missed him terribly, her mother had reacted with silence and a cold detachment. George knew that this was because his sister and his brother-in-law had not loved each other for some time. His sister, Mary, had told him this in letters.

Herbert George had received many letters over the

years from his sister, but since Delilah's father's death more letters had been coming from his niece. Several months ago she had written to her uncle telling him she wanted to move away from the East and asking him for a job. George had readily agreed, because he loved his sister, and he loved his niece, even though he had not seen her since she was five. He hardly expected the young woman who walked into his office and hugged him tightly.

Now, months later, she was standing in front of him, looking at him with disapproval.

"Stop glaring at me and sit down," he said.

She sat.

"What is it, Del? What's bothering you?"

"You told me Clint Adams had agreed to be interviewed," she said.

"Oh," he said sheepishly, "that."

"Yes, that. I was very embarrassed, Uncle Herbert."

"Look, Del, he was playing hard to get. I thought you might be the one to get the interview from him given his, uh, reputation with women."

"All I know about him is what I read in the East, and what you told me, but after this morning I don't think he's that kind of man."

"What kind of man is that?"

"The kind that he has a reputation for being."

"He talked to you?"

"A little."

"Did he agree to do an interview?"

"No."

"Did he ask to see you again?"

She hesitated, then said, "Yes."

"When?"

"Tonight, for dinner."

He slapped his palm down on his desk top and said, "I knew I was right. He'll give you the interview, Del."

"I hope so," she said. "I'm tired of writing obituaries, Uncle Herbert."

"If you get this interview, you won't be writing them much longer."

In spite of herself she felt excited at the prospect of getting to do some real writing.

"I'll get the interview, Uncle Herbert," she said, standing up, "but for the record I don't like being deceived and embarrassed."

"Even if it means getting the interview?" he asked.

She stared at him somberly for a few moments, and then had to laugh.

"Yes," she said, "even if it means getting the interview. I want to be a reporter, Uncle, but I want to have integrity, as well."

He scowled and said, "You learned that from your mother, didn't you, girl?"

"Yes, I did."

"Well, here in Denver we'll try and knock that idealism out of you."

"You won't," she said. "I won't let you."

As she went out the door, he said, "Pigheaded as your mother, too," but he couldn't tell if she heard him.

After Delilah Perkins left the club, Clint got an idea, but he knew it was one he'd have to keep to himself. If Bat—or Talbot Roper, for that matter—knew what he was doing he'd never hear the end of it.

First, though, he had to get away from Bat Masterson.

"I thought you were doing paperwork."

"I got tired of it. I thought I'd go around and talk to some people about Talbot Roper. Want to come?"

"I don't think so," Clint said. "I think I'll get some rest before my dinner engagement tonight."

"You'd better keep your eye on that one, Clint," Bat said. "She's a smart one."

"Good," Clint said. "I like them smart."

"And the fact that she's pretty doesn't hurt either, huh?" Bat asked.

After Bat left, Clint headed up to his room to change clothes and then went back down to hail a cab in front of the club. He gave the driver the address before climbing into the back. The ride didn't take long. He got out, paid the man, and approached the building. Before entering he read the plate that was affixed to the outside wall:

PINKERTON AGENCY

TWENTY-THREE

Clint presented himself to Allan Pinkerton's secretary, not at all sure that Pinkerton would see him. He had sort of the same relationship with Pinkerton that Talbot Roper had. There was respect there, but Pinkerton was too straight-laced while Roper and Clint were—in Pinkerton's words—too "irreverant."

The secretary went into Pinkerton's office and returned two minutes later.

"Mr. Pinkerton will see you, Mr. Adams."

"Thank you."

"Go on in. Would you like some coffee?"

The offer surprised Clint. Apparently Pinkerton was in a mood to entertain.

The secretary was in her early fifties, an extremely handsome woman dressed very sharply.

"Thank you."

"How would you like it?"

"Black, and strong."

"I'll bring it in."

Clint nodded and went through the open door of Pinkerton's office.

Allan Pinkerton, looking pink, portly, and prosperous, stood up behind his desk as Clint entered.

"Clint Adams," he said. "It's been a while."

"Allan," Clint said.

"What are you doing in town?"

"Visiting friends."

"Talbot Roper?"

"He's one," Clint said. "Also Bat Masterson."

"Ah yes, I must confess," Pinkerton said, "I read Mr. Masterson's column."

"Do you also read Earl Klinger's column?"

"I beg your pardon?"

"Klinger, the crime columnist."

"Well, yes, as a matter of fact I do read Klinger's column."

The secretary came in carrying a tray with a silver coffeepot and two china cups.

"None for me, Meredith," Pinkerton said.

"Yes, sir."

She poured Clint a cup, handed it to him on a saucer, then left the tray on the desk and walked out.

"Why don't you sit down, Clint, and tell me what's on your mind."

Clint sat down, balancing the cup and saucer on his knee.

"It's about the murders, Allan."

Pinkerton studied Clint for a few moments then asked, "Are you speaking about the prostitutes?"

"I am."

"What do you know about it?"

"Nothing, until I arrived here yesterday morning. I've read as many newspaper stories as I could since then."

"For what reason?"

"Curiosity."

"Yes," Pinkerton said, "I can believe that of you, Clint."

"What do you know about them, Allan?"

Again Pinkerton took his time before answering. He leaned forward and poured himself a cup of coffee.

"I can understand how your curiosity might be aroused by these murders, Clint, especially since he's struck twice in the past two nights. That's a definite break in his previous pattern."

Clint smiled.

"I was right to come here," Clint said. "You've been following the case closely, haven't you?"

"I admit, I have," Pinkerton said, "just in case someone decided to call us in."

"Then you haven't been called in?"

"No."

"Not even to consult?"

"No," Pinkerton said, squirming in his seat. "I'll tell you something I haven't told anyone else."

"What?"

"I got in touch with Chief Farley and offered my services and the services of my operatives."

"And he said no?"

"Emphatically," Pinkerton said, his face turning red at the memory. "In fact, he was quite insulting. Have you met the man?"

"I have."

"Then you know what I mean. He is not the most

personable man you would ever want to meet."

Clint bit his tongue. Up until this very meeting he would have said the same thing about Allan Pinkerton.

"What's your interest in this case, Adams . . . I mean, really?"

Now it was Clint's turn to hesitate. He leaned forward and deposited the cup and saucer on the desk. The coffee was untouched.

"I'm not really sure myself, Allan. Maybe it's in the stories I read."

"What do you mean?"

"These murders are pretty brutal, and they're being perpetrated against women. That just doesn't sit right with me."

"And you want to do something about it?"

"Let's just say I wish I could do something about it," Clint answered. "I'm not sure there is actually anything I can do."

"Were you hoping that I would, indeed, be working on it?"

"I suppose I was."

"It really isn't the kind of thing we'd work on, you know. This kind of . . . violence is often best handled by the police."

"I realize that."

"Still, I guess I feel much the same way you do. I wish there was something I could do."

"Isn't there?"

Pinkerton gave Clint a look.

"I was warned off quite firmly by Chief Farley. He told me in no uncertain terms that if I interfered I'd be out of business."

"That doesn't sound like the kind of threat you'd knuckle under to, Allan."

"Well, maybe I'm getting old."

That was the first bald-faced lie Clint caught the man in since his arrival, but he did not say anything. Instead he stood up, preparing to leave.

"I doubt that, Allan."

"It's true. I'm even thinking of retiring and letting my son, William, run the whole show."

"I'll believe that when I see it."

Clint started for the door.

"That's all?" Pinkerton asked.

"That's it." Clint turned to face Pinkerton again. "I just thought I'd see what you knew, or how you felt about these murders. Frankly, Allan, I'm surprised you agreed to talk to me."

"As I said before, Clint," Pinkerton said, "I must be getting old."

Sure, Clint thought as he walked out, but not too old to lie.

After Clint left Pinkerton's office, the man called his secretary back in.

"Yes, sir?" She frowned at the untouched coffee. Meredith Tyler hated waste.

"Get me Jeff Spanner."

Every year or so Pinkerton managed to get himself a new top man in his agency. This year it was Jeff Spanner, a former army officer who had started working for him just a few months ago.

"Yes, sir."

She started to pick up the coffee and put it on the tray.

"Do that later, Meredith. I want Spanner here within the hour."

"Yes, sir," she said, reluctantly leaving the pot and the cups, "within the hour."

TWENTY-FOUR

Clint took a cab back to the club. During the ride he wondered why Pinkerton had lied to him so poorly. Allan Pinkerton would not retire until they carried him out of his office in a box. Anyone who believed less did not know the man.

The lie could only mean one thing. He'd lied earlier, as well. That led Clint to the only conclusion he could come to. Somehow, in some way, Allan Pinkerton was looking into the murders.

When Clint arrived at the club, he no longer saw any reason to keep it from Bat that he'd seen Pinkerton. He would not, however, tell Roper—at least, not until everything was said and done.

As he entered the lobby he suddenly became aware that it was past lunchtime. He'd be meeting Del for dinner, but that wouldn't be for a few hours yet. Instead of going to his room he turned right and went into the dining room.

The young waiter, Dave, came running over as soon as he saw Clint.

"A table, Mr. Adams?"

"Doesn't look like there are any, Dave."

"Mr. Masterson said you were to use his table whenever you were here, sir."

"Oh, well, that's all right then. Lead the way."

Dave took Clint to Bat's table and took his order for lunch. As the waiter walked away, Clint noticed Earl Klinger standing in the doorway. He knew two things. One, Klinger wasn't going to get a table, and two, he'd been banned by Masterson. Clint debated his next move, but decided to make it anyway. He stood up and waved until the man saw him, then waved him over. Klinger crossed the room to him. Clint thought briefly that the man Bat had banned was now going to have lunch at Bat's table, but he could reconcile that later.

"Hello, Earl—uh, can I still call you Earl away from the poker table?"

"If I can call you Clint," Klinger said.

"No problem. Why don't you sit?"

"Thanks."

"There aren't any other tables, and I didn't know how hungry you were."

"Well, actually," Klinger said, "I didn't come for lunch, but now that you mention it I am kind of hungry."

"The waiter will be back shortly, and he can take your order. If you're not here for lunch, Earl, then why are you here?"

"I was looking for you, or Bat."

"What for?"

"Just a talk."

"About last night? Frankly, I'm surprised to see you here after that."

"To tell you the truth, I don't remember a whole lot about last night, Clint."

"How much do you remember?"

"Well, I remember being banned, and I think I called Bat a cheater."

"Well, you insinuated that he was a cheater, but you're right about being banned."

"Well, was I banned from the poker game or the club entirely?"

"I believe it was the club," Clint said, "but I guess I can check with Bat on that for you."

"That's all right," Klinger said. "I should talk to Bat myself."

"To apologize?"

"Uh, yeah, well there's that."

"What else is there?"

"Well, I've heard what Bat's had to say about the killings of these prostitutes."

"So?"

"I was wondering if he planned to do anything about it," Klinger said. "I was also wondering the same thing about you."

"Me? What could I do?"

"You and Bat have the biggest reputations in Denver, Clint. What if one or both of you let it be known, in the newspapers, that you were looking for this killer? What do you think would happen?"

"Nothing. Why, what do you think would happen?"

"Well, if I was the killer and I heard that Clint Adams and Bat Masterson were after me, I'd hightail it out of town."

"You would, huh?"

"Don't you think he would?"

"Frankly, no."

"Why not?"

"Because he's a killer, Earl. Killers are crazy, and they're arrogant, especially ones like this."

"What do you know about killers like this?"

"Over the years I've dealt with all kinds of killers."

"But like this?"

"There was one like this in London, England, a few years ago when I was there for a gun expo."

"So you don't think he'd be afraid of you?"

"Anything but. In fact, if we did what you say it might incite him to more daring murders."

"Couldn't be much more daring than last night, could it?" Klinger asked. "It looks like he killed her right on the street then dragged her into an alley."

"Could the street have been that empty?"

"That street could," Klinger said. "The good women of Denver call it 'Prostitute Square.' "

"The good women?"

Klinger frowned.

"That's what they call themselves."

"What do you think is going on, Earl?"

"What do you mean?"

"Well, I haven't been here very long, but it doesn't seem to me that the police are trying very hard to find this killer."

"You want my personal take on this?"

"That's what I'm asking for," Clint said. "I want what you haven't written in your column."

Klinger thought a moment, and in that time Dave came back.

"Will you be having lunch with Mr. Adams, sir?"

"Yes," Klinger said, "I'll have whatever he's having."

"Very good, sir," Dave said. "I'll bring it along."

As Dave left, Klinger addressed himself to Clint's question.

"First of all," he said, "we've got us a bad chief of police."

"How did he get the job?"

"Politics. He's a good politician, but a bad policeman. In fact, he isn't even a policeman. A lot of us thought that Bill Wilkins would get the job."

"Wilkins?"

"He's a captain with the police department. He's been with the department ever since it started its present incarnation."

"And what happened?"

"Farley got appointed from the outside."

"By who?"

"Mayor Johnson."

"And what were his qualifications for the job?" Clint asked.

"That's it, as far as I can see," Klinger said. "He knows the mayor."

"How long has he had the job?"

"A year."

"What's the mayor think now?"

"Damned if I know," Klinger said. "He doesn't talk to me."

"Does he talk to your boss?"

"Probably."

"What does he say?"

"Herbert and Mayor Johnson are friends, Clint. He doesn't tell me about his conversations with the man."

"Have you asked him?"

"No."

"Maybe you should."

"I like my job."

"I thought you and George were close."

"Who told you that? Bat?"

"He . . . mentioned it."

"Well, he's wrong. Herbert would fire me in a minute if he wanted to. As long as people read my column, though, he won't."

"Are you worried about Bat and his column?"

Klinger firmed his jaw.

"You and Masterson are friends, Clint. I don't want to say anything against him, especially not when you're buying me lunch at his table."

"You and Bat aren't friends then?"

"Acquaintances."

"Colleagues?"

Klinger made a face.

"You don't think much of Bat as a writer, do you, Earl?"

"Can I answer that honestly and still eat lunch?"

"Sure, go ahead."

"He's got no business writing on the same paper with me."

"Then why is he?"

"Because he asked Herbert for the job and Herbert gave it to him."

"Would he do that if he didn't think Bat could write?" Clint asked.

"He would do whatever he thought he had to do to sell newspapers."

"What about the people who read Bat's column and enjoy it?"

"What about them?"

"They buy newspapers."

Klinger remained silent.

"They probably read your column as well," Clint went on. "Where's the harm in you and Bat at least being friendly rivals?"

"I don't think you can use the word friendly in reference to us, Clint . . . especially not after last night."

"You've got a point there, Earl. I think you'd have to apologize."

"I don't know if I could do that."

"Why do I think you're as stubborn as Bat?"

"I'm stubborn," Klinger said, "but I don't know how I compare to Bat in that respect."

"Take it from me," Clint said, "you match him."

The waiter returned with their lunches and set the steaming plates down in front of them.

"I'll tell you one thing, though," Klinger said.

"What's that?"

Chewing, Klinger said, "I hope I'm only barred from the poker game and not the club."

"Why?"

"I think Bat might just have himself the best cook in Denver."

"I'll talk to him," Clint said.

TWENTY-FIVE

The killer spent the day quietly. He knew that he had crossed the line killing two women so close together. He shouldn't have allowed liquor to fuel his temper, and then his temper to fuel his hunger, and so on. . . . He was going to have to be careful from here on.

He started to read the newspaper account of last night's killing with lunch, but then put it aside. Even reading about it fueled the hunger, which was like a fireball in his stomach.

He knew that he had the police baffled. They didn't know where to look for him, and they weren't getting much help from their chief of police.

The killer had known, one year ago, when Farley was hired that the man would be inept at the job. It was funny, but it was when Farley got the job that he first started to get the hunger. He was able to fight it off for a long time, but finally it had become too strong.

He picked up the newspaper and started reading the reports again. What did it matter if it fueled the hunger? He could probably kill as many women as he wanted and the police wouldn't be able to stop him.

Maybe, he thought, he'd even be able to graduate from whores. They were, after all, filthy women who deserved to die. What would happen if he killed a so-called "decent" woman? What would the reaction of the city of Denver be? Could there be a man among them who didn't know that all women were filthy creatures?

This time he read the newspaper account all the way through, then put aside the *Post* and read *George's Weekly*. By the time he finished that one he could feel the burning in his stomach. He knew he had to do something. He put the newspaper aside. If he didn't stop the burning it would grow and grow until it ate away his insides.

He had to do something.

"Waiter!"

The nearest waiter turned and looked.

"A cold beer, quickly."

"Yes, sir."

He closed his eyes and tried to calm himself. Even though he knew he was safe, that the police couldn't possibly catch him or stop him . . . and if that was the case, why worry about . . . no, he'd already taken too much of a chance with the last woman . . . but he *was* untouchable, wasn't he?

Wasn't he?

He stood up and took out his wallet.

"Sir?" the returning waiter said. "Your beer?"

"That's all right," the killer said. "I don't need it now."

He paid his bill—including the beer—and hurried out, leaving behind the puzzled waiter, holding a full mug of ice-cold beer. Finally, the man drank it himself.

After all, it was paid for.

TWENTY-SIX

After lunch Earl Klinger thanked Clint and said he had to get back to the office.

"Earl," Clint said, "somebody should be asking questions."

"Of whom?"

"Chief Farley. Maybe even Mayor Johnson."

"And you think it should be me?"

"Who better than a newspaperman?"

"If that's the case," Klinger said, "why don't you make the same suggestion to Bat?"

Klinger turned and left without waiting for an answer.

"Was everything all right, sir?" Dave asked.

"Everything was fine, Dave. What do I owe you?"

"Nothing, sir."

"Nothing?"

"According to Mr. Masterson."

"Well, take this, then," Clint said, handing him some money for a tip.

"Oh, sir, I can't—"

"This'll just be between you and me, all right, Dave? There's no reason for Mr. Masterson to know anything about it."

"Well . . . all right, then. Thank you, sir."

"Sure, Dave."

Clint left the dining room and went out to the lobby. Once again he started for his room and stopped. Lunch had whet his appetite for a beer. He went into the bar, which was much less crowded than the dining room.

"What can I get for you, Mr. Adams?" the bartender asked.

Clint didn't remember being introduced to the man, but the staff of the club had obviously been alerted as to who he was.

"A cold beer would be nice."

"Comin' up."

Clint looked around the room but didn't see anyone he had been introduced to. Some of the men, however, were looking at him curiously, so it was apparent they knew who he was.

It gave him an uncomfortable feeling. He was used to be recognized, but not used to having everyone in the room know who he was. It made him feel inadequately armed with just the little Colt New Line nestled against the small of his back.

"Mr. Adams?"

He turned and looked at the bartender.

"Your beer, sir."

"Thanks. What do I—"

"On the house, sir."

"Thanks."

He turned again to regard the room, this time because he didn't feel comfortable giving it his back. In fact he didn't even want to be standing. He walked across the room and sat at a table against the back wall.

He was starting to think that if everyone in the goddamn building was going to know who he was, he might be better off going to a hotel. He didn't know how Bat did it, day in, day out. Then again, Bat wasn't as preoccupied with being shot in the back as Clint was. He hadn't been close friends with Wild Bill Hickok when it had happened to him in Deadwood. That was probably the single incident in Clint's past that had affected him the most. The effects were twofold. First, he missed his friend, and second, he felt that he was probably going to end up the same way.

He nursed his beer, pushed Wild Bill Hickok out of his mind, and thought instead about present-day things, like the murder of five women. Why, he wondered, had the man killed so soon after the fourth one? Had whatever was driving this man become so unbearable that he just had to do it again?

Why was he so fascinated by what was happening? It seemed to him to be more than just simple, normal curiosity. He had, after all, come simply for a visit with Bat. Why get involved beyond that?

He wondered how Bat was faring with his attempt to put together some sort of committee that would pay Talbot Roper's fee. He was obviously going to solicit money from the more wealthy citizens of Denver. It was not the wealthy who were being killed, though, it was street whores. Would the rich of Denver be willing to pay money to stop the killing of the poor? Would the rich in any town or city be willing to do that?

Probably not, he thought, and that was a shame.

He watched a man walk across the room toward him. Well-dressed, soft-looking, his body was not built for the expensive clothing he was wearing. High forehead, sandy hair, thinning, cheeks that looked like he never had to shave. He was probably in his thirties. He stopped in front of Clint, holding a drink in his hand.

"Mind if I join you?"

Clint was about to say yes, he did mind, when he realized that he was sitting in a men's club, where the members associated with each other.

"Sure, why not?"

"Thank you."

The man sat down and took a few moments to make sure he was comfortable before looking at Clint again. He had a surprisingly deep voice.

"My name is Clayton, Royce Clayton."

"Clint Adams."

"Yes, I know. That's the reason I came over to talk to you."

"What can I do for you, Mr. Clayton?"

"Nothing, really," Clayton said. "I just wanted to sit and chat with a famous man."

"I'm not a famous man, Mr. Clayton," Clint said, shaking his head. "The President of the United States, now there's a famous man."

"I've met the President, Mr. Adams. If you'll excuse me for saying so, he's quite boring. You, on the other hand, are doubtlessly not."

"What do you do, Mr. Clayton?"

"Me? I don't do much of anything, sir. You see, I am quite wealthy. I don't *have* to do anything."

Clint decided to put his questions to this man.

"Mr. Clayton, do you mind if I ask you a question?"

"No, I don't mind at all. Ask away."

"I assume you read the newspapers?"

"Every day."

"Then you know about the women who are being murdered."

"Oh, yes, quite shocking. One can only be thankful that . . . decent women aren't being killed."

There it was, the attitude he had just been thinking about.

"Don't you think it should be stopped?"

"Oh, definitely."

"What would you be willing to do to stop it?"

"Me?" The man blinked and stared at him blankly. "What should I do?"

"Oh, I don't know. Let's say you could pay a certain amount of money and the killings would stop. Would you?"

"Why should I?"

"Well, because as you said, you're very rich. You wouldn't miss a few dollars, and then there wouldn't be any more dead women."

"Yes, but . . . these women are common whores. I mean, it's not like honorable women are being killed."

"All right," Clint said, "let's say honorable

women *were* being killed. Would you pay then?"

Royce Clayton thought this question over very carefully, then peered across the table at Clint and asked, "Would I know any of these women?"

TWENTY-SEVEN

Clint left Royce Clayton sitting in the bar without saying another word to the man. He found himself so angry at the man's attitude—even though he had expected it—that he thought it best to simply leave.

He was coming out of the bar into the lobby, finally heading up to his room, when Bat Masterson came in the front door.

"Whoa," Bat said, "if looks could kill, somebody would be dead right now. Who is it?"

"Royce Clayton."

"Clayton?" Bat said. "Why would you let that foppish asshole upset you?"

"Because he proved a theory of mine."

"Theory about what?"

"The killings."

"Ah. Is this a theory you'd like to share?"

"I'm too angry right now. Can we talk later?"

Bat looked at his watch, then said, "Okay, that's fine."

"What about you?" Clint asked. "How did you do today?"

Bat made a face but he said, "I'll tell you about that later, too."

"Okay," Clint said. "I'm going up to my room. I haven't been back since this morning."

"What have you been up to?"

"I'll tell you," Clint said, "later."

They parted company there, Clint going to his room and Bat to his office.

In the bar Royce Clayton sat in his chair, staring at the chair recently vacated by Clint Adams. He had an amused twinkle in his eyes, a slight smile on his face. He knew exactly what Clint Adams was feeling when he stood up and walked out without a word. It was a feeling a lot of people got when they talked to him. He knew just how to look and what to say to *make* them feel that way.

He finished his drink, then stood up and started across the room toward the lobby. The men sitting at tables along the way turned their heads or averted their eyes, anything not to attract Clayton's attention. He knew they were thinking, God, he's such a bore, don't let him sit down and talk to us.

Little did they know . . .

TWENTY-EIGHT

Clint woke up late from an afternoon nap and realized he wouldn't have time to talk to Bat before he had dinner with Delilah Perkins. Maybe he and Bat could update each other after his dinner date.

He immediately removed his clothes, washed himself using Bat Masterson's new "modern" facilities (How soon, he wondered, before this sort of indoor plumbing became normal?) and then dressed again in clothes suitable to having dinner with a young lady. He paused with the Colt New Line in his hand, then decided to simply drop it into his pocket rather than tuck it in against the small of his back again. That done, he left the room and went down to the lobby.

There was no sign of Delilah yet, so he decided to go to Bat's office to tell him he couldn't talk to him until later tonight. Besides, he hadn't yet seen his friend's office.

He followed directions Bat had given him the first time he arrived and knocked on an unmarked door.

"Come in."

He opened the door and entered. Bat was sitting behind a big wooden desk. On the desk was a hand of solitaire.

"Busy man," Clint said.

"It helps me think," Bat said.

Clint closed the door behind him and looked around. The room was large and sparsely furnished. If Bat was ready to stay there a long time, wouldn't he have furnished it more?

"Black jack on red queen."

"I see it."

Clint smiled.

"You're looking sharp," Bat said, looking up. "Ready for dinner with Delilah Perkins?"

"I believe so."

"She's gonna get that interview out of you."

"I don't think so."

"What are you gonna get out of her?"

"None of your business. Red seven on black eight."

"I see it."

"We can talk when I get back, okay?"

"Or in the morning," Bat said, with a chuckle.

"You have a dirty mind," Clint said, heading for the door.

"It's not dirty," Bat called back, "it's just active."

Clint opened the door, said, "Red three on black four," and left, just barely able to hear Bat yell, "I saw it!"

• • •

His timing was perfect. When he reached the lobby, Delilah Perkins was just walking in. She saw him and smiled. She had the kind of smile that transformed her face from cute to pretty. She was wearing a simple green dress with a neckline that stopped just short of showing cleavage, and she was carrying a shawl.

"Delilah."

"Ready, Clint?" she asked.

"You look wonderful, and yes, I'm ready. Where would you like to go?"

"I get to pick?"

"It's your city," he said, as they went out the door.

"Hardly," she said. "I've only been here a few months, but I do have some favorite places to eat."

"Then you get to pick," he said. "I haven't been here long enough to find favorite places . . . just favorite people."

"Oh, Mr. Adams," she said, shaking her head, "I can see you're going to be a dangerous man."

TWENTY-NINE

They got a cab and Delilah gave the driver an address. Clint didn't pay any attention to it. He was watching her. He saw that she could very easily have been a beautiful girl, but she took her looks for granted. She wore no makeup, preferring to look natural, and with her green eyes and flashing, infectious smile she *was* naturally beautiful—in an understated sort of way.

"Do I have a wart?" she asked.

"What?"

She laughed.

"You were staring."

"Oh, I'm sorry . . . but you must be used to being stared at."

"Not really," she said. "I'm not that sort of girl."

"What sort is that?"

"The sort that men stare at."

116

"Why do you say that?"

"Because it's true."

"Why do I get the feeling you almost never look around you?"

"What do you mean?"

"Don't you know you were being watched in the lobby back there?"

"Oh yeah," she said, "by who?"

"By everyone. Delilah, you're a lovely girl, the kind men like to look at."

She touched her face, looking thoughtful for a moment, then dropped her hand to her lap and said, "Oh, Clint, you had me going for a moment."

He decided to give up for now. She obviously had no idea of her own appeal, and he wasn't going to convince her of it in one cab ride.

When they reached the restaurant, Clint was impressed. They were met at the door by a man in a tuxedo who showed them to their table and gave them elaborate menus to read and order from.

"I forgot to tell you," she said. "The *Weekly* is buying dinner tonight."

"I can buy dinner," he said.

"I know that," she said, "but I didn't want you to think I took you to an expensive restaurant just to . . . you know . . ."

"Why would I have thought that?" he asked, eyeing the prices on the menu. This was easily the most expensive restaurant he had ever been in.

"Well, we'll just let my uncle's money buy this one dinner, all right?"

"Delilah—"

"No argument?"

He hesitated a moment, then said, "No argument."

"Good."

"But a condition."

"What condition?"

"Eating this meal does not mean I'm agreeing to an interview."

She smiled and said, "Understood. Shall we order now?"

Over dinner Clint had Delilah tell him all about herself and her life in the East before she moved to Denver. She had been devastated by her father's death, and then by her mother's reaction. It was more the latter that drove her to move.

"It was as if she didn't feel it, you know? Like she didn't miss him."

"How long were they married?"

"Thirty years."

"Maybe she didn't miss him."

"What?"

"Maybe after all that time she liked the idea of being alone."

She stared at him for a moment and then said, "That's crazy."

"Why?"

"They were married, for Chrissake," she said. "Devoted to each other."

"How long can that keep up?"

"As long as it can. Have you ever been married?"

"No. You?"

"No, but I can tell you that when I do get married it will be forever."

He could see that she was adamant about this. It was why she couldn't forgive her mother for her feelings.

"How old are you?" he asked.

"Twenty-five."

He didn't say anything.

"Aren't you going to tell me that I have a lot to learn?"

"Why?"

"That's what Uncle Herbert always tells me."

"Then you don't need me to tell you, do you?"

"No."

"Then I won't."

"Thank you."

"Besides, I don't think you need anyone to tell you that."

"Oh? Why not?"

"Because you're a smart woman, Delilah."

She stared at him.

"Most men would have said a smart *girl*."

"Would you call me a boy?" he asked.

"Certainly not."

"Then I won't refer to you as a girl."

"What is wrong with this picture?" she asked, sitting back in her chair and staring at him.

"What do you mean?"

"I mean—" She stopped short, and when she continued he had the feeling it wasn't what she was originally going to say. "I mean it seems as if you're interviewing me."

"I'm not," he said, "I'm just trying to get to know you."

"Well, now," she said, "if I try to get to know you, will you think I'm interviewing you?"

"I don't know," he said. "Will it involve a notebook?"

"No," she said. "Just talk."

"There's not much for me to say."

"You're joking. With the life you've led?"

"The life I've led . . ." he said, letting it trail off.

"What's wrong?"

"I made some bad choices years ago, when I was about your age, and I ended up leading the life that I've led."

"And you're not satisfied with it?"

"No," he said. "I'm not."

She stared at him for a few moments, then said, "Clint, I promised my uncle I'd try to get you to agree to an interview."

"I'm not surprised."

"What I want to tell you now, though," she continued, "is that if you want to talk to me it will be strictly off the record."

He smiled and said, "We are talking, Delilah."

"No, I mean if you have something you . . . you really want to say."

He knew what she wanted. She wanted him to confide in her, to tell her things that he wouldn't tell anyone else. Clint didn't really have anyone in his life like that, and on such short acquaintance he certainly wasn't ready to make Delilah Perkins that person.

He looked at her and asked, "Would you get offended if I said I don't think so?"

She stared back at him for a few moments, then said, "No, no, I wouldn't. After all, we don't know each other all that well, do we?"

"Not yet."

"At least," she said, "not for the kind of conversation I was talking about."

He reached across the table, covered her hand with his, and said, "Let's keep it light, shall we?"

She smiled and said, "Sure . . . for now."

THIRTY

After dinner they had coffee. He had a piece of pie and she a dish of ice cream. She looked very much like a little girl, spooning vanilla ice cream into her mouth, but she wasn't. While at twenty-five there were still vestiges of the girl in her, she was very much a woman. Her uncle was right, though, she did still have a lot to learn, but Clint knew that she knew it, too.

After dinner they went outside and she suggested they take a walk.

"Can we walk back to the club?"

"No," she said, "but from here we can walk to my room."

That surprised him, but he said, "All right."

If there was ever any doubt that Delilah Perkins was a woman, it was dispelled that night.

She seemed to get shy as they walked up the steps

to her room. When she tried to put the key in the lock, her hand shook slightly. He steadied it with his, and they fitted the key into the lock together.

Inside she turned to face him.

"I'm nervous."

"Why?"

"I haven't been with a man since . . . well, since I came here."

"That hasn't been so long."

"Well, I . . . it goes back longer than that."

"You're not a virgin, are you, Delilah?"

"No," she said, "I'm not . . . but I haven't been with a lot of men."

"That's nothing to be ashamed of."

"You've been with a lot of women, haven't you?"

"Over the years," he said, "there have been women."

"Special ones?"

He smiled.

"All women are special in one way or another. Look at you."

"What about me?"

"You're very smart, you're a decent person, you're modest—"

"I'm not so modest, I just know—"

"Unassuming, then," he said. "You have a—"

"Would you just kiss me?" she asked. "Stop telling me what I am, and who I am, and just kiss me."

He kissed her. She was tentative at first, but then her mouth opened. She tasted sweet, like ice cream. He touched her face and her neck and found her skin smooth and hot. He kissed her neck, and then her throat, and her chest as far as he could before he reached behind her, opened her dress and let it slip from her. He removed her underwear and she stood there naked, but somehow no longer shy. The look in her eyes was pure woman now, hungry and slightly wanton.

He kissed her again, lips, neck, throat, and then kissed her breasts, teasing her nipples with his lips and tongue but not using his teeth. He didn't know why he had the feeling she'd be sensitive, but she was. Biting her might have hurt her, but she responded eagerly to the touch of his fingers, his lips, his tongue.

When he got to the blond hair between her legs he found it fine, almost wispy. He allowed it to tickle his face, and then probed with his tongue. She moaned and spread her legs for him, leaning down and bracing herself with her hands on his shoulders. She was certainly not a virgin, for this was nothing new to her. She gasped when his tongue touched her, and he slid his hands up the back of her thighs until he was holding her by her shapely buttocks.

"Oh God," she said as a shudder went through her, "I can't . . . my legs . . ."

He knew what she meant. Her legs were weak. He stopped what he was doing, stood up, and looked around.

"The bed is in the next room," she said.

"Then let's go there."

"First," she said with a smile, "leave your clothes here."

He smiled back and undressed while she watched him with obvious pleasure. Once they were both naked they walked together to the other room. . . .

•   •   •

The first time they made love it was gentle, a learning experience. They both knew what to do, but they had to find out what they could do together. It was fun, as Clint felt sex should be.

He learned that her nipples were exquisitely sensitive, that he could make her shudder and cry out just by licking them gently, but constantly.

She learned that he liked it when she took him in her mouth and sucked him slowly, moving her mouth up and down his length until it was almost like sweet torture.

Later they made love with more urgency. He slid his hands beneath her to cup her buttocks and drove himself into her. She lifted her hips to meet each of his thrusts with one of her own, crying out each time.

Later, as they lay side by side, she said, "I'm going to be sore tomorrow."

"I'm sorry."

She laughed.

"I didn't mean for you to apologize," she said, slapping his thigh. "It will be a wonderful sore. Every time I feel it I'll think of you, and then I'll want you. People will wonder what I'm thinking about when they see the look on my face, and they'll never know. It's just for me to know."

"And me."

She turned over so she could press herself against him. He slid an arm around her and her breasts flattened against his side. She put her hand on his belly. She was not as small-breasted as she appeared when she was dressed. He had known women like that before, whose appearance when dressed actually hid their true figure. She was still slender, but her breasts were round and firm.

"Just because I said I'll be sore, though," she said, kissing his chest, "doesn't mean that we're all finished."

She was licking his nipples, circling them with her tongue, as he said, "I didn't for one moment think it did."

THIRTY-ONE

Clint found Bat in his office early the next morning. This time Bat was dealing out phantom hands of poker.

"Winning?" Clint asked.

"Of course," Bat said. "I always win."

"Got time for breakfast?"

"Sure." Bat gathered the cards together and put the deck in his top drawer.

On the way to the dining room Clint asked, "Why is it I never see you working on this column of yours?"

"Nobody sees me doin' that," Bat said. "That's a private thing."

"Oh."

"Did you ever write anything?"

"Letters."

"You know what I mean."

"There was a publisher in Boston a while back that

wanted me to write my life story."

"And?"

"I decided not to do it."

"Why?"

"Because it's private."

"Oh."

When they were seated at Bat's table and had ordered breakfast, he said to Clint, "You didn't make it back last night."

"No, I didn't."

"Did you give her that interview?"

"No, I didn't."

"Did you give her anything?"

"There goes that active mind of yours again."

"Well, you missed the poker game last night. I was just hoping it was worth it."

"The poker game," Clint said. "Your regular Friday night game."

"Yes."

"I forgot all about it. How'd it go?"

"Well, I won."

"No, I mean, who showed up?"

"The regular players."

"Chief Farley?"

"He wasn't there."

"Earl Klinger?"

"He's not a regular player. Besides, I banned him, remember?"

"I meant to ask you about that."

"What about it?"

"Is he banned from the game, or from the club entirely?"

"How the hell do I know?"

"Well, you banned him."

"I know, but I did that on the spur of the moment. I don't remember if I banned him from the game or the club. I tell you what, you pick."

"Me? Why me?"

"Because you think straighter than I do. I get emotional."

"Okay," Clint said, "then he's banned from the game."

"Why the game? He was never a regular player."

Clint gave Bat an exasperated look.

"You asked me to decide. If you were going to argue with me, why ask me?"

"Okay, okay," Bat said. "So he's banned from the game, but not the club."

"Okay."

"Okay."

Bat waited a beat and then said, "I heard he was here yesterday."

At that moment Dave arrived with the coffee.

"Benedict Arnold," Clint said, looking up at the young man.

"I beg your pardon, sir?" Dave said.

"Never mind, Dave. Thanks."

As Dave left, Bat said, "Of course he told me. He tells me everything."

"I'll remember that."

"Why? What else are you gonna hide from me?"

"Nothing. I wasn't hiding anything from you this time."

"Then why didn't you tell me he was here?"

"I have to tell you who I have lunch with?"

Bat stroked his chin.

"No, I guess not."

"What is with you and Klinger, anyway?"

"He doesn't like me, so I don't like him."

"Well, gee, that sounds perfectly fair, doesn't it?" Clint asked.

"Yeah, it does."

"Did you ever think to sit down and talk to him for a while?"

"What for?"

"Well, for one thing if you and he became friends he could help you with your writing."

"I don't need help with my writing."

Clint didn't reply.

"What's wrong with my writing?"

"I don't know what's wrong with your writing," Clint said. "What do I know about writing? I'm just trying to find a solution for this . . . feud."

"There's no feud," Bat said. "We're just not . . . friends."

"Well, you write for the same paper, he comes to the club, he played poker with us—"

"And called me a cheater."

"Come on, Bat. He was frustrated and drunk."

"Nobody calls me a cheater."

"This is not the old West anymore, Bat. You don't shoot a man for accusing you of cheating at cards."

"And I didn't, did I? I just banned him from playing with me again."

"Well . . . that's good enough, I guess."

"Can we stop talking about Earl Klinger now?"

"Sure."

"After you tell me what he was doing here yesterday."

"He said he was looking for you or me."

"Well, he found you, so what did he want?"

"He had a suggestion for us."

"What was it?"

Clint hesitated a moment, then told him.

THIRTY-TWO

Over breakfast Bat actually said, "It doesn't sound like a bad idea."

"It's a terrible idea," Clint said.

"Why?"

"Because it won't make the killer leave town."

"But," Bat said, holding up a fork with a piece of egg on the end of it to make a point, "it will tweak his nose, especially if I write in my column that I think he's afraid of us."

"In your column?" Clint asked. "You have a sports column, Bat."

"I have the freedom to write about anything I please. Why do you insist on thinking this is a bad idea?"

"Tell me what you think it will accomplish."

"It might make the son of a bitch come after us, and then we can do what the police haven't been able to do."

"Bat," Clint said, leaning forward, "this man kills women. Do you know why he kills women?"

"How the hell should—"

"Because he can," Clint said. "Because they're easy prey for him. Men are *not* easy prey for him, and you and I will certainly not be easy prey for him."

"So if he's not going to leave town and he's not going to come after us, what do you think would be accomplished by doing this?"

"He'll kill again. Maybe more frequently."

"More frequently than now?" Bat asked. "My God, man, he just killed two nights in a row."

Clint sat back in his chair. He knew he had a point, but he also knew that Bat did, as well.

"We're sitting here arguing about the behavior of a crazy man," Clint said.

"Right," Bat said. "Nobody knows what he's gonna do next, so why don't we just go for it?"

"How are you going to get this by your publisher?" Clint asked.

"Are you kidding? Herbert will love it."

"Bat," Clint said, "the idea was Earl Klinger's."

"What are you suggesting?"

"That we do this in his column."

"Why?" Bat's expression was not a happy one.

"Because this killer, whoever he is, might not read your column, but he probably likes reading about himself, and he probably does that in Earl's column."

Bat didn't reply.

"If you really want to do this just to stop these killings, you won't worry about whose column it's in."

"All right, damn it," Bat said. "All right. We'll do it in Earl's column."

"Then we better go and talk to George today," Clint said.

"Right after breakfast," Bat said.

"It's a crazy idea," Herbert George said. He looked at Clint and asked, "Do you really think this has a chance to work?"

"What are you asking him for?" Bat demanded. "Why don't you ask me?"

"Clint's an outsider," George said. Then he looked at Clint and said, "Sorry, I meant no offense, it's just—"

"I know what you mean, George. No apology necessary. Do I think it will work? I don't know. Like I told Bat, we're trying to predict what a crazy man will do next. It can't be done."

"Are you willing, though?"

"Sure, I'm willing," Clint said. "If it will keep this guy from killing any more women, I'm willing."

George looked at Bat.

"You know I've got to clear this with Farley, don't you?"

"Farley? Why? What will he care?"

"He might not," George admitted, "but I've got to talk to him about it anyway."

"You gonna let him talk you out of doin' it?" Bat asked.

"No, I'm not, Bat."

"Good."

"This was Earl's idea, you say?"

"Yes," Clint said, before Bat could say anything. "He told it to me yesterday."

"He didn't say a word to me," George said.

"I think it should be done in his column," Clint

said. "Sort of like him quoting me and Bat."

"Almost like a challenge," Bat said.

"And you think he'll come after you?"

"Clint doesn't think so," Bat said, "but I think he might."

"And if he does?"

"Denver won't have him as a problem anymore," Bat said.

"And if he doesn't come after you?"

Bat looked at Clint, who looked at Herbert George and shrugged.

"Who knows?" he said.

THIRTY-THREE

Klinger wasn't around so Herbert George said he'd talk to him when he came in.

"I'll let you know tomorrow when we're going to do it," he said.

"You better make it soon, Herbert," Bat said. "Who knows when this maniac will strike again?"

"Tomorrow," George said, "will be soon enough."

Outside the newspaper office Bat said, "Where the hell is Klinger when you want him?"

"He's probably out looking for the killer."

"Speaking of looking for the killer," Bat said, "what should we tell Roper about this?"

"Speaking of Roper," Clint said, as they flagged down a cab, "how did you do raising money?"

"Not as well as I would have liked."

"How many people did you get?"

They stepped into the cab and gave the driver the address of the Olympic Club.

"How many?" Clint asked again.

"None."

"None?"

"None of the people I approached were interested."

"You approach people with money, naturally."

"Naturally."

"People like Royce Clayton?"

"Well, not Royce Clayton, but yes, people like him."

"Those people aren't going to be interested in saving some street whores, Bat."

"I know that now."

"So what will you do? Foot the bill yourself?"

"No," Bat said, "I expect that you and I and Frank Quay can handle it."

"Quay," Clint said. "Why didn't I think of that before? He could probably pay the entire fee with no problem."

"Probably," Bat said, "but would it be fair to ask him to do that?"

"Is it fair to ask me? I don't even live here."

"That never stopped you from helping people before," Bat said.

"I know, I know . . ."

"Well," Bat said, "I guess there's no harm in seeing what Quay says to the idea."

"As far as what Roper will think of the column idea," Clint said, "he won't like it, but we can't get in touch with him now. We'll just have to go ahead and explain it to him later. Meanwhile, we'll have to at least pay his retainer today."

"Well, when we get back to the club I'll try to locate Frank. I can probably get him to put up that much with no problem. It's the final fee we'll have to worry about." Bat frowned. "We'll take care of that when the time comes."

"There's something else I ought to tell you," Clint said.

"What's that?"

"I went to see Allan Pinkerton yesterday."

"Why?" Bat asked, just mildly surprised. "He hates you."

"Well, he was very civil yesterday," Clint said. "I wanted to find out what he thought about this killer, and if he was interested in the case at all."

"You were gonna hire him when we can't even pay Roper's fee?"

"No, I didn't want to hire him," Clint said, "I just wanted to pick his brain a little."

"And what fell out?"

"Lies."

"What do you mean?"

"He started to talk about retiring."

"Pinkerton?"

"He started talking about getting old."

Bat nodded and said, "He was lying."

"And he said that these killings were not his kind of case and that they were better handled by the police."

"Lying."

"He also told me, in confidence, that he offered his services to Chief Farley, who turned him down and warned him off—rudely."

"Farley wouldn't be rude to Pinkerton," Bat said, "he'd be too intimidated."

"More lies."

"So Pinkerton is looking for the killer," Bat said. "But why?"

"Simplest reason."

"Someone hired him."

"Right."

"Who?"

"I don't know."

"Guess."

"I can't," Clint said. "You live here, you guess."

"Somebody with money, obviously. He's even more expensive then Roper."

"Okay, figure this," Clint said. "The people you talked to today turned you down because they— some of them—have already banded together and hired Pinkerton."

"That's a possibility."

"Did you tell them what you wanted? Specifically?"

"I didn't mention Roper, if that's what you mean. I just talked about joining forces and hiring someone to find this maniac."

"And they said no? Just like that?"

"Not just like that, but they said no."

"And no one mentioned Pinkerton?"

Bat looked at Clint and said, "I think I'd remember that."

THIRTY-FOUR

There was nothing else to be done that afternoon and evening. They had to wait to hear from Herbert George the next day.

"The bar?" Bat asked.

"Let's go and talk in your office," Clint said.

"Why there?"

"I'll tell you when we get there."

They pulled up in front of the club and got out, and were immediately accosted by Royce Clayton, who was also going in.

Most of the men who frequented the club considered being spoken to by Royce Clayton as being accosted.

"Bat. Mr. Adams," Clayton said.

Bat hunched his shoulders because he recognized the voice without looking at its owner.

"Royce," Bat said. "Good afternoon."

"Hello, Mr. Clayton," Clint said.

"Please," Clayton said, "call me Royce."

"All right, Royce."

The three of them started inside together.

"May I buy the two of you a drink?" Clayton asked.

"I'm sorry, Royce. We were just heading to my office to take care of some business. Maybe later."

"Of course, of course," Clayton said. "Anytime would be my pleasure."

In the lobby Clint and Bat quickly veered away from Clayton and headed for Bat's office.

Once inside with the door closed, Bat walked around behind his desk and sat down. He immediately took the deck of cards from his desk drawer.

"Pull your chair closer," he said.

Clint pulled the chair close to the desk. Bat immediately started dealing a hand of five-card draw. Clint received a pair of deuces—diamond and club suit—along with a nine and ten of clubs, and a queen of hearts.

Bat dealt himself an ace and king of clubs, a jack of hearts, a nine of hearts, and an eight of spades.

"How many cards?"

Clint kept his deuces and drew three cards. Bat kept the ace and king of clubs and drew three, also.

"You never told me why Clayton made you so mad yesterday," Bat said.

"He's a heartless son of a bitch. I asked him about using his money to help those women and he wasn't the least bit interested." He also told Bat what Clayton had said when he asked if he would want to help "decent" women.

Clint looked at his cards. The hand was pretty, but it hadn't improved. He still had deuces, along with an ace, a three, and a four of hearts.

Bat had made a pair of kings.

"Kings," Bat said.

"Deuces."

"This is no fun without betting," Bat said.

"So we'll bet," Clint said.

They both took out money and an impromptu two-handed poker game began, and went on for hours, during which they discussed many things. At one point Bat even went out and got Dave and told him to keep coming in to check and see if they wanted drinks.

There's a theory in poker that says if two people play long enough they will eventually come out even. Clint and Bat were going to test that theory for the next ten hours.

THIRTY-FIVE

Nine and a half hours later Clint was holding a pair of fives—hearts and spades—with a deuce and seven of spades and an eight of clubs.

Bat had a jack of clubs, a ten of hearts, and a three of hearts along with a five and nine of diamonds.

True to the theory, they were about even after all this time, even though the stakes had kept going higher and higher. They'd started betting dollars and the last pot was over four hundred dollars, which had gotten Clint close to even.

They both decided to test their luck.

Clint kept the three spades, discarding a pair and thereby breaking a cardinal rule of poker. Still, you had to take a chance sometimes.

Bat kept the five and nine of diamonds and began to think very hard—or pray very hard—for the six, seven, and eight. He'd pulled this very same hand in a game once, but only once.

So much for luck.

Clint's first card was a nine of spades, giving him hope, but the second card was a five of clubs. If he'd kept the pair of fives he'd now have three of them.

Bat made king high and disgustedly tossed his hand in. Clint raked in the pot and was now a hundred dollars ahead.

"What time is it?" he asked.

Bat looked at his watch and said, "Midnight."

"What?" Clint thought that couldn't be right. "We've been playing for . . ."

"Almost ten hours."

"I don't believe it."

Bat counted his money and said, "I'm a hundred dollars down."

"All that effort for a hundred dollars?"

"What effort?" Bat said. "We've been passing money back and forth while we try to solve the problems of the world."

"I'll settle for one problem in particular."

"Back to that again," Bat said. He gathered up the cards and said, "Let's do what we did with Klinger the other night?"

"Deal out seven cards, faceup?"

"Yeah."

"For how much?"

Bat thought, then said, "Two hundred. That way we won't finish even. Somebody will win."

"Okay," Clint said, "go ahead."

"After this I'm going to bed," Bat said, shuffling the cards. "Begging people for money all day and being turned down is tiring work."

He dealt the cards.

First card Clint got was a seven of diamonds.

Bat got a ten of clubs.

Second card: three of spades to Clint, three of clubs to Bat.

The third card Clint received was a four of spades. Bat made a three of diamonds for a pair of threes.

"Hah," he said, "pair of threes."

"Keep dealing, Masterson."

Clint got a ten of spades, and now had three spades with three cards to go.

Bat got a seven of spades, which did nothing to improve his hand.

"Want to give up now?" Bat asked.

"Deal."

The fifth card Clint got was a four of diamonds, which gave him a pair of fours.

Bat's card was a five of hearts, no help.

"Hah," Clint said, "got you beat."

"Sixth card comin' out," Bat said. "Watch it and weep."

Clint got a jack of spades, giving him four spades. Bat got an ace of clubs.

It was still Clint's fours against Bat's threes.

"Last card," Bat said, "comin' out."

Clint got a nine of hearts, which meant he still only had fours.

Bat did not deal his last card out.

"Come on, deal," Clint said.

"Want to double the bet?"

"What for?"

"Well," Bat said, "if you lose I could put the money toward Roper's retainer—which, I might add, we were supposed to pay today."

"Until we got involved in a ten-hour, two-handed poker game," Clint said. His tone said that such a game was insanity, but then he and Bat had done it before. "Come on, deal," he said.

"What about the bet?"

"I tell you what," Clint said. "If I win you won't ask me for the money to pay Roper."

"And if I win?"

"I'll chip in."

"How much?"

"I'll match whatever you put in."

Bat thought for a moment, then said, "Deal."

He dealt the last card.

He got an ace of diamonds, giving him aces and threes.

"Ah," he said, "I should have made you double your bet."

Bat took the pot. He was now a hundred dollars ahead, plus he had Clint on the hook for part of Talbot Roper's fee.

THIRTY-SIX

When they came out of the office, they ran into Dave coming the other way.

"We're through for the night, Dave," Bat said. "Thanks."

"Someone was here from the newspaper, Mr. Masterson," Dave said.

"Oh? Who?"

"A man named Carlson."

"You know him?" Clint asked Bat.

"Not well, but I know he works for the paper. Why didn't you send him to the office, Dave?"

"I thought you and Mr. Adams were busy."

"We were just passing the time, Dave," Bat said. He supposed he should take some of the blame. He should have told Dave that there was no reason they couldn't be interrupted.

"What did he want?"

"He had a message from Mr. George."

Dave stopped there. Sometimes Bat thought that the young man was as smart as he was ever going to be, which wasn't saying much.

"Well, what was the message?"

"He said to tell you that something you talked about would be in the paper tomorrow."

"Yes," Bat said, looking at Clint. "I told you, George is not one to waste time."

"You know what he meant?" Dave asked.

"Yes, Dave, I do. That's all. You can go home now."

"I was just wondering."

"Go home, Dave!"

"Yes, sir." Dave scurried off like a puppy that had been kicked.

"Sometimes I wonder why I keep him around."

"Because he thinks you can walk on water, that's why."

"Listen," Bat said, "once Klinger's column appears tomorrow we're going to have to be joined at the hip. We'll have to watch each other's backs."

"You really think the killer will come after both of us if we're together all the time, Bat?"

"You've got a point. What do you suggest?"

"I think one of us has to play bait, while the other one covers him discretely."

"Discretely, huh?"

"Right."

"And which of us do you suggest plays the bait?"

"You."

"Me? Why me?"

"Because I can keep a low profile and you can't. You live here, and everyone knows who you are."

Bat scowled and said, "Leave it to you to come up with a logical reason."

"Well," Clint said, "we could play one hand of poker for it."

"Forget it," Bat said, "I had my share of luck tonight. I'd probably lose anyway. Okay, I'll be the bait, but if you let me get killed I'll never forgive you."

"I'll keep that in mind."

THIRTY-SEVEN

The next morning Bat sent out for the newspaper early and then met Clint in the lobby.

"Let's go in the dining room and read it," he said.

"How about your office?" Clint asked. "It's more private."

"Clint, the paper just came out," Bat said. "I don't think our man has had time to decide what he wants to do. Besides, I'm hungry."

"Okay," Clint said, "so am I. Let's go."

They went into the dining room and sat at Bat's table. A waiter came over to take their order, and it wasn't Dave.

"What happened to Dave?" Bat asked.

"He didn't come in today, Mr. Masterson. I guess he must be sick."

"Or crushed," Clint said, and Bat gave him a hard look.

"What's your name?" Bat asked the waiter.

"Walter."

"Well, Walter, bring us some coffee and—"

"You want your usual breakfast, Mr. Masterson?"

"You know what I eat for breakfast?"

"Oh, yes, sir."

"Okay then, bring two."

"Yes, sir."

As the waiter left, Bat looked at Clint.

"Don't say it."

"What?"

"About Dave."

"I'm not saying anything."

"If he doesn't come in tomorrow, I'll try and find out why, but we've got other things to worry about."

"Let me see the column," Clint said.

"I haven't read it yet."

"Why didn't you get two copies?"

"Wait, here it is: 'This reporter has been told by Bat Masterson that he and his friend, Clint Adams, also known as the Gunsmith, think that this killer of women is a coward. They say they are going to take to the streets and do what the police cannot do—rid Denver of this maniac.'"

Clint waited for more, and when it didn't come he said, "That's it?"

"That's it about us. He goes on to wonder what the chief of police is going to think about this."

"I wonder, too."

"We probably won't hear from him," Bat said. "What's Roper gonna think?"

"If he sees it, I don't know what he'll think. I know one thing, though. We better get over to his office today and leave his retainer with his secretary."

"We'll do that after breakfast."

"And then we'll decide just how we're going to dangle you as bait for this killer."

"Carefully," Bat said, "very carefully."

The killer read the column again, then put the newspaper down very gently. His movements belied the rage he felt, but he was in a public place and couldn't afford to be noticed.

Who did they think they were? How could they say that about him in the newspaper, for everyone to read? Didn't they realize what a service he was doing for this city, cleaning up the streets?

What could he do about it? He felt the hunger, the burning, start in his stomach. This was going to be their fault, this time. He had decided not to kill again so soon, but now he had to do it just to show them that they couldn't scare him, not when he was on a mission. What kind of a man would he be if he let them scare him off?

He picked up the newspaper and read the column again, because each time he read it, it was like throwing coal on a fire.

THIRTY-EIGHT

Clint and Bat dropped by Roper's office to leave the retainer with Dolores, his secretary. As they entered, she looked up from her desk. They were still reorganizing the office, but it wasn't quite as messy as it had been a couple of days ago. In fact, at the moment she was reading the newspaper.

George's Weekly.

Earl Klinger's column.

"I don't think Mr. Roper's going to like this," she said.

Neither Clint nor Bat answered.

"I mean, I haven't worked for him that long, but I don't think he's going to like this."

Clint and Bat exchanged a glance.

"We don't like it, either," Clint said.

"We don't know where he got that information from," Bat said.

She stared at both of them.

"Can I help you?" she finally asked.

"Yes," Bat said, "we want to leave Mr. Roper's retainer with you."

"You were supposed to bring it yesterday."

"I know," Bat said.

"Have you heard from Tal?" Clint asked.

"No," she said, "not since that day, the day you hired him."

"Then he's working on the case," Bat said.

"I believe so," she said.

Clint took an envelope from his pocket and handed it to her.

"The retainer," he said.

"Yes," she said, setting the envelope down on the desk.

"Don't you want to count it?"

"I have strict instructions not to," she said.

At least not in front of them, Clint thought.

"Is that all?" she asked.

"Yes," Clint said, "that's all."

She looked down at the newspaper, then back up at them.

"He's not going to like this at all."

"I still say he might not even read the newspaper." Clint said. "Besides, we're friends. I can make it right with him."

"We can only do that by paying him," Bat said. "When we get back I'll talk to Frank Quay. Between all of us, we should be able to handle it."

They were in a cab on the way back to the club. Clint felt like all he'd been doing since he arrived was eating and riding in cabs.

"I just got an idea," he said.

"What?"

"We need to go and look at the area where the girls are being killed."

"Why?"

"Two reasons," Clint said. "One, maybe he'll see us there, and two, I just want to see it for myself."

"Today?"

"Now," Clint said, "while we're out."

Bat leaned forward and stuck his head out the window. The wind took his voice away, but Clint knew he was giving the driver the location.

Clint wasn't sure why he wanted to walk around the area, he just felt that they should.

"Okay," Bat said, "we're on our way. Are you armed?"

"Of course."

Clint knew that Bat had a gun in a holster under his arm.

"Maybe we'll get lucky and get this over with today," Bat said, touching the gun.

"Maybe," Clint said.

THIRTY-NINE

When they reached the area, Bat told Clint it was called Foley Square.

"Why?"

"I don't know," Bat said. "From what I understand, last year it was called Grant Square, and the year before Walker Square. I guess nobody wants to lay claim to it."

Clint didn't know why. In the daylight it looked like any other slightly run-down part of a town or city. There were shops, some cafés, some saloons. There were people walking the streets, but they looked like working people, not street whores or their pimps.

"The whores come out at night," Bat said. "This place transforms when it gets dark."

"Do you know where the girls were killed, where they were found?"

Bat shrugged and said, "Alleys, that's what I heard.

Wait, that last woman was killed on the street." Bat looked around, getting his bearings, then said, "I think it's this way."

They walked a block and a half and then Bat stopped.

"Here."

Clint looked around and saw a brownish stain on the sidewalk. Some had even dripped between two cobblestones in the street.

"He killed her here and then took her where?" Clint asked.

"This way," Bat said.

Clint had a feeling that Bat had been paying more attention to particulars than he let on.

He followed Bat to an alley.

"This is where they found her."

Clint stepped into the alley and looked at the ground. More brown stains but lighter, like someone had tried to wash it away. He came out of the alley and looked around.

"What do you see?" Bat asked.

"He could be watching us from any of these buildings," Clint said.

"You think so?"

"It's possible."

"But what? What's going on inside your head, Clint? I can see your mind working."

"I think he comes here to kill the girls," Clint said, "but I don't think he's here otherwise."

"Why not?"

"From what I've read he's very precise, he doesn't make a mess."

"You call cutting up women not making a mess?"

"He doesn't do it messily," Clint said. "One article

I read even wondered if the man was a doctor."

"Well, if he is, he doesn't have an office here."

"Whether he is or isn't, I don't think he lives here, either. I don't think he'd want to kill so close to home."

"So why is he killing here?"

"Because this is where he can find the kind of women he wants to kill."

"Whores."

"Street whores," Clint clarified. "If he wanted a whore he could go to some of the high-class saloons and clubs and find very clean ones. No, he wants to kill *these* girls in particular."

"Why?"

Clint shrugged.

"Maybe because they're dirty."

"Your mind is scary," Bat said.

"Why do you say that?"

"Because I wouldn't have thought of any of that," Bat said, "and it sounds like it makes sense."

"Now the question is, what do we do about it?" Clint asked.

"He's not gonna come after us, is he?" Bat asked.

"I don't think so, Bat. In fact, I think he'll go after another woman."

"Here?"

"Here."

Bat looked around and said, "Well, I guess here is where we should be, huh?"

"I think so."

"But where?" Bat asked. "And when?"

"Tonight," Clint said. "He'll do it tonight."

"Why?"

"Because he's already killed two of them close together. Reading Klinger's column is going to push him over the edge. He's going to want another one, Bat, tonight."

"You feel sure about this?"

"For some reason I do, yeah," Clint said.

"Okay," Bat said, "then that's what we'll do. If we're comin' back later, though, I'm gonna want more firepower."

"Yeah," Clint said, thinking about the gun and holster in his room, "so am I."

They left the alley and started walking back to where they could pick up a cab. People they passed along the way stopped and stared at them, and for just a moment Clint thought a man looked familiar to him.

"What is it?" Bat asked.

"Nothing, nothing," Clint said. "I just thought I recognized someone."

"Who?"

"I don't know," he said. "We passed a man who looked a little familiar."

Bat turned but he didn't know which one Clint was talking about.

"Forget it," Clint said. "Let's get a cab, get back to the club, and make our plans for tonight."

The man Clint and Bat had passed, who Clint thought was familiar, turned and watched from a doorway as Clint Adams and Bat Masterson got into a cab. He didn't know what they were doing there, but he had a feeling they would be back.

When their cab left he stepped out of the doorway, looked right and left, then started walking toward the alley Clint and Bat had just come out of. As he entered the alley a figure stepped from behind some boxes, and before the man knew what had happened he felt a sharp pain in his stomach as a knife punched its way through his clothes and his belly.

The man with the knife pulled it free and allowed the other man to fall right on the exact spot where they'd found Katy Miller.

The killer stepped out of the alley and looked up and down the street. This man had been here all day. The other two, Masterson and Adams, would probably be back that night. He'd be waiting for them, too.

FORTY

When Clint and Bat got back to the club, Bat said, "Let me check the bar for Quay."

Clint followed him to the entrance of the bar.

"Frank's here," Bat said. "He's at the bar."

They entered and walked to the bar where Frank Quay was standing, talking to three other men.

Quay saw them approaching and excused himself from the men he was talking to.

"Hello, Bat, Clint," he said. "Buy you fellas a drink?"

"You can buy more than that, Frank," Clint said.

"What?"

"Let's start with a beer," Bat said, putting his elbows on the bar.

Delilah Perkins knocked on her uncle's door and entered. He sat back in his chair and studied her.

"When you knock, it means you want something," he said. "What is it?"

"I want to work on the Foley Square killings."

"Impossible."

"Why? Because I'm a woman?"

"No—"

"Because I'm your niece?"

"That's not—"

"Then why?"

"Because you have no experience."

"Well, how am I going to get experience if you never let me work on anything?"

"I gave you the Adams interview."

"He doesn't want to be interviewed."

"Make him want to. That's your job."

"Uncle Herbert—"

"That's all, Delilah," Herbert George said. "If you don't want to do that I've got some more obituaries you could write."

"No," she said quickly, "no more obituaries."

"Then get out of here and do your job."

She firmed her jaw, said, "Yes, sir," and left his office. It took all of her will not to slam the door.

She stalked across the floor, dodging desks and leaving puzzled looks in her wake. She was wearing an expression no one at the paper had ever seen on her before.

Do your job, her uncle had said. Well, as far as she was concerned, she had come here to be a reporter. *That* was her job, and if her uncle wanted her to do her job, well that was all right with her.

On her way out he passed Earl Klinger coming in.

"Hey!" he called. "Where's the fire?"

"Foley Square," she said.

"What?"

But she didn't answer. She kept right on going, out the door and away from the building.

Klinger went running upstairs to see what they knew about a fire in Foley Square.

FORTY-ONE

Clint and Bat waited until it was fairly late—after nine o'clock—to leave the club and head for Foley Square. Both were wearing their guns in holsters on their hips. On the way out, though, they ran into Earl Klinger coming in.

"Oh, I'm glad I caught you," he said.

"What is it, Earl?" Clint asked. Bat just looked at the man without speaking.

"I thought you'd want to know that they found a man stabbed in Foley Square."

"What?" Clint said.

"He stabbed a *man* this time?" Bat asked, shocked.

"If it's the same guy, yeah, he did."

"Did he mutilate him, like the women?" Clint asked.

"That's just it," Klinger said. "The victim is still alive."

164

"Did he see who stabbed him?" Clint asked.

"I'm on my way to the hospital right now to find out," Klinger said. "The police won't tell us anything but the man's name."

"And what is his name?" Clint asked impatiently.

"Roper," Klinger said, "Talbot Roper."

"I swear I didn't know you knew him," Klinger kept saying as the three of them shared a cab to Denver Hospital.

"It's okay, Earl," Clint kept saying.

When they reached the hospital, they had a problem with a policeman who was sitting outside of Roper's room.

"Nobody goes in," the man said.

"I'm a friend of his," Clint said.

"I'm sorry, but nobody can—"

"Is he conscious?"

The policeman stared at him.

"You can tell me that, can't you?"

"Yes, he's conscious."

"Why don't you go in and tell him that Clint Adams is here?" Clint asked. "He'll want to see me."

The policeman thought it over, then went inside. He returned within two minutes.

"Well?"

"He knows you."

"So, can I go in?"

"I could get into a lot of—"

Earl Klinger stepped in then and took over. Apparently he'd had some experience getting past troublesome policemen.

"Have you ever been in the newspaper?" he asked.

"Me? No, I haven't—"

"Well," Klinger said, taking the man by the arm and leading him down the hall, "we should make sure I have the right spelling of your name. What *is* your name?"

"Smith."

"Well," Klinger continued as Clint entered Roper's room, "there are a lot of ways to spell Smith . . ."

Roper was alone in the room. He was lying on his back with his eyes open, his face pale.

"Tal?"

He focused his eyes on Clint.

"What were you and Masterson doing down in Foley Square today?" was the first thing he said.

"Never mind that," Clint said. "What happened to you?"

"He caught me unawares, Clint," Roper said. "He was in that alley where you and Masterson were."

"The alley? When?"

"This afternoon," Roper said. "At the same time you were."

"I didn't hear him or see him."

"Neither did I," Roper said, "until he stuck me."

"Did you get a look at him, Tal?"

"I sure did."

"Who was he?"

"I never saw him before in my life."

"Can you describe him?"

"He was a big man. Not muscular, but big and bulky. He moved fast and quiet for a man his size."

"Did he say anything?"

"Not a word. He just tried to kill me."

"Why didn't he, I wonder?"

"I don't know. It would have been easy enough to finish me."

"Tal, do you think he knew who you were?"

Roper thought that over for a moment.

"It's possible, I guess," he said. "I have been in the newspaper, probably too many times. I might have to make some changes in the way I operate . . ."

This last was an aside, as if he was speaking to himself. Clint realized that the man was starting to fall asleep. He also realized that it had been Roper he'd seen that afternoon, when he told Bat that a man they'd passed had looked familiar. The private detective had been in disguise. Was it a coincidence that the killer had picked him?

"You take care, Tal," Clint said. "I'll come back and see you tomorrow."

Eyes fluttering, Roper said, "Get the son of a bitch for me, Clint. Get the son of a . . ."

"I will, Tal," Clint said. "I'll get him."

Clint left the room and Bat grabbed him by the arm.

"We have to get to Foley Square!"

"I know, Bat, but—"

"No, I mean now. Fast!"

"What are you talking—"

"Tell him," Bat said to Klinger.

"It wasn't my fault," Klinger said. "I didn't know what she meant."

"What who meant? What are you talking about?"

"I saw Delilah Perkins earlier today. She was going out of the building as I was coming in. She was in such a hurry that I asked her where the fire was—you know, kidding? She said Foley Square."

Clint and Bat looked at each other.

"I went upstairs to see if there really was a fire—"

Clint and Bat didn't hear the rest. They were running down the hall. . . .

FORTY-TWO

Delilah Perkins was thinking, This is what it's all about, being a reporter.

She was in Foley Square, walking the streets with the other women. She had found some old clothes, a low-cut dress, and had corsetted herself into it so that her bosom was thrust up and out. She just knew that if she bent over her breasts would fall out. This was her idea of what a Foley Square street whore looked like. In point of fact, she looked better than most of them. After the first half hour she thought maybe she'd overdone it. Other girls had already been approached and gone off with their customers. She was starting to think that maybe she looked too expensive. She thought maybe she should rub a little dirt on her face and bosom, but what man would want her then?

She continued to walk around the square, swinging her hips back and forth. The heels on the shoes she was wearing were making her feet start to hurt. Suddenly she stopped short and looked around. She realized that it was very late and she was the only woman on the street. How had that happened?

She looked around herself nervously. It was as if it had just occurred to her where she was and what she was doing. If she came face-to-face with the killer, what was she going to do, interview him? She couldn't even get a wonderful man like Clint Adams to submit to an interview.

Her heart started to pound and she decided she wanted to go home. She turned around and gasped. There was a man standing there, all dressed in black and wearing a cape. She hadn't heard him come up behind her at all.

"H-hello," she said hesitantly.

He didn't answer.

"I was, uh, just going home for the night. I'm sure one of the other, uh, women would be glad—"

"There are no others, luv," the man said.

"I, uh, well, you see, I'm not really a—"

"Come on, now, my dear. It will only hurt for a moment. Don't make it harder on yourself."

"Oh no . . ." she said, staring at him in horror.

The moon was out and it glinted off the blade as he brought it out from beneath his cape.

"No!" she shouted and started to run.

She ran as fast as she could, but she could hear his footsteps right behind her. She imagined that she could feel his hot breath on her neck, and she dared not turn around to see how close he was.

As she ran she wanted to scream, but it seemed to take all of her breath just to keep running. Every time she opened her mouth to yell or scream, nothing came out but gasps.

That was all she could hear—footsteps, and her own gasps for air—along with the pounding of her heart in her ears.

She needed help, but the square was empty. Her terror-filled eyes searched for a way out, an open doorway, or an alley. Something, anything that would offer her refuge. She did not even dare to slow down to pound on a door, for fear that he would be able to lay his hands on her.

Why hadn't she stayed writing obituaries?

FORTY-THREE

Clint and Bat leapt out of the cab when it reached Foley Square. They already knew they were going to split up and look for Delilah, and that's what they did. The driver called after them to see who was going to pay his fare, but they both ignored him. Plenty of time to find him later and make it up to him. What they had to do now was save a young woman's life.

Clint ran through his part of the square, which appeared to be empty. He swept the area with his eyes and then decided it would be smarter just to call out for her.

"Delilah!"

His voice echoed and there was no reply.

"Delilah!"

He became dimly aware of another voice calling and realized that it was Bat calling her name, as well. If he could hear Bat, she should certainly have been able to hear him.

"Delilah! Answer me!"

There were a few moments of echoing, followed by silence, and then, finally, he heard her.

"Clint!"

Delilah couldn't believe her ears when she heard her name. She tried to answer, but couldn't. Her throat was constricted now not only by fear but by the dryness that was there as a result of the running and gasping for air.

She heard her name again, and again, and then suddenly there were hands on her, grabbing her, pulling her, squeezing her, and squeezing a scream from her tortured throat.

"Clint!"

Delilah's voice echoed, and Clint stopped running immediately. He instinctively felt that he was not going to get another chance, that she would not have another chance to yell. He was going to have to wait for the echoes to fade and then take his best guess.

"Who's out there?" the man asked her, with his hand clamped over Delilah's mouth. "Is that Clint Adams?"

Of course, she couldn't answer. She wasn't sure she could have spoken even if he removed his hand.

"Yes, yes," the killer said, "that is the famous Clint Adams. The man who thought he could stop me by putting his name in the newspaper."

Oh, God, she thought, find me, Clint, please find me. . . .

"I wonder if he has Bat Masterson with him, hmm? Do you think so, my dear?"

Oh, God, was all she could think.

"Let's find out, shall we?" he said.

Clint was still trying to make his guess when he saw them. The man was clad in black with something flowing around him—a cape—and he held the girl in front of him. Delilah had dressed herself up in her idea of what a street whore would wear. If she wasn't moments from death it might have been comical.

They stood there for a moment, frozen in time it seemed, and then he was dragging her off down the street.

"Bat!" Clint began shouting, even as he started after them. "Bat, I found them! Bat! Bat!"

He thought only briefly of firing a shot, but was afraid that would cause the man to kill her. He even stopped shouting for that reason.

He just kept running after them.

Bat stopped short when he heard Clint's voice. It came again. He'd found them, but where were they? Someplace behind him. He turned and started running back the way he'd come, following the sound of Clint's voice until it stopped. After that, he just kept running.

Jesus, Clint thought, the man was strong. He was running with Delilah and her feet weren't even touching the ground. This man did not seem to match the description of the man who had stabbed Roper. He was fast, yes, but he did not appear to be bulky.

The man was strong, for sure, but carrying Delilah

was slowing him down. Clint was closing ground, and the man knew it.

And suddenly they were gone. Just like that. Disappeared.

Clint kept running, and when he got to the point where they had vanished he saw the alley, the same alley Katy Miller had been killed in, the same one where Talbot Roper was stabbed. It seemed to be an alley that the killer liked quite a bit.

Clint looked both ways and to his left he saw Bat Masterson. He waved him over. If he was going to go into this alley, he'd damn well rather do it with Bat Masterson watching his back.

FORTY-FOUR

"Where'd they go?" Bat asked. He was out of breath when he reached Clint.

"There's only one place they could have gone," Clint said, equally out of breath. He pointed.

"That's the same alley," Bat said.

"I know."

He drew his gun at the same time Clint did.

"Let's do it," Clint said.

"I'm going to take my hand away from your mouth," the killer said to Delilah.

She didn't believe it.

"When I do," the man said, "I want you to scream."

She thought it was so odd that the man had such a pleasing odor about him. His body, his breath, everything was pleasant. Also, he had the prettiest accent she had ever heard.

"Do you understand?"

She didn't, but she nodded her head.

"Good."

He took his hand away.

"Scream."

She opened her mouth and tried to, she really did, but nothing came out.

"Come on, my dear, if you don't scream they might just turn around and leave you to me. Scream."

She tried again, but her throat was so dry and tight that nothing came out.

"Oh, dear," the man said, "I see I am going to have to help you along."

She didn't know what he meant until she felt the tip of his knife bite into her side. My God, he was killing her!

She screamed.

Clint and Bat were already on their way into the alley when they heard the scream.

"Easy," Bat said. "He wants us to rush in."

"I know."

Out on the street there was the light of the moon, but the interior of the alley was as black as coal. They stepped into the darkness, then paused to let their eyes adjust.

"He's trapped," Bat said. "He won't kill her while he needs her."

Clint nodded, but he wondered who was really trapped, them or the killer. The man obviously felt secure in this alley.

After a few moments their eyes were able to make out shapes in the alley and they started further in.

"Keep coming, gentlemen," the killer's voice said in an accent Clint recognized as English.

Clint and Bat moved forward, shoulder to shoulder. They were cautious, because although most of the damage inflicted by the killer to this point had been done with a knife, they had no way of knowing if he was otherwise armed.

"Surely your eyes must be adjusted to the darkness by now, gentlemen. Can you see us?"

The killer had his back against a brick wall and was holding Delilah directly in front of him. He was wearing a hat with the brim pulled down so that his face was hidden.

"I have a knife pressed against the young woman's side," he said. "In fact, I believe I've already pricked her with it."

"What do you want?"

"Do I have the pleasure of addressing Messrs. Adams and Masterson?"

"You do," Bat said.

"Gentlemen, I wish to offer you a—what do you call it here? A deal."

"What kind of deal?" Clint asked.

"I have no desire to, er, cross swords with you."

"We've got guns, friend," Bat said. "What do you have?"

"I have a knife, Mr. Masterson, and as I said, it is pressed against this lovely young woman's side."

"What's the deal?" Clint asked.

"I wish to take my leave of your city, perhaps even go home."

"To England?" Clint asked.

"You have a good ear, sir."

"Why should we let you go?" Bat asked. "We have you trapped."

"I have the young lady," the killer said. "You can

have her if you let me go, and I shall not bother your fair city again. I believe I have worn out my welcome here."

"You're a killer," Bat said. "We can't let you go."

"Actually, you don't have much choice in the matter," the killer said. "I shall be leaving shortly. I just wanted you to know—specifically you, Mr. Masterson, as you are, among other things, something of a journalist—that I'm leaving. I'm finished with you. You shall not hear from me again."

"I have a question before you go," Clint said.

"I will answer it if I can."

"Why did you stab that man earlier today?"

"I beg your pardon?"

"The man you stabbed today—"

"I did not stab a man today, gentlemen. On my honor."

"Then who did?" Clint asked.

"I seem to have picked up a protector along the way," the killer said, "a follower, you might say. If you find him, perhaps he can tell you."

"Who is he?" Clint asked.

"Ah, that's for you to find out," the killer said. "As for me, I now bid you farewell."

Suddenly, Delilah was pushed toward them and they both went to catch her. Clint allowed Bat to hold her as he stepped forward, only to be met by the wall.

"Where did he go?" Bat asked.

"I don't know," Clint said, touching the wall with his hands.

"Over?" Bat asked.

"I don't see how."

He continued to probe the wall, following it until

he suddenly came to an opening—a slender opening.

"This must be it."

Bat came closer and saw it.

"I can't fit through there," he said, patting his stomach.

"I can," Clint said, "but I'm not going to."

"Why not?"

"He's gone, Bat."

"Maybe we can catch him."

"No," Clint said, "I mean, he's gone."

"You believe him? What he said about leaving for good?"

"Yes, I do."

"But—"

"Come on, I think he cut Delilah. We've got to get her to a doctor."

"I hate to let him go," Bat said.

Clint shook his head and said, "I do, too, but at least he's gone, and I'm glad."

"I guess that remains to be seen," Bat said, still unconvinced.

FORTY-FIVE

Clint stayed in Denver another week. The prize-fight went off as planned and was a huge success for Bat. Jimmy "King of the Ring" King was still King of the Ring.

Talbot Roper was not as badly wounded as had originally been thought. There was no internal bleeding, and he was actually able to attend the fight.

Also in attendance was Delilah Perkins. Her injury was minimal. The killer's knife had pricked her just enough to draw some blood and make her scream. What made her feel better was that Bat did an article for the *Weekly* about the killer, and wrote it with Delilah, sharing the byline. In the same issue of the paper Earl Klinger did his own story, and the paper did very well.

After the fight Clint, Bat, Roper, Delilah, and Frank Quay all went to the bar. They were sitting at a table when a man in his thirties approached and asked for Clint and Bat.

"You're looking at them," Bat said.

"My name's Jeff Spanner, I'm a Pinkerton operative."

"Congratulations," Bat said, unimpressed.

Clint was kinder.

"What can we do for you?"

"I just wanted to congratulate the two of you," Spanner said. "I was working on the case for Mr. Pinkerton for a while, and I came up empty. Apparently, your methods were better than mine. I was wondering if we could talk about it."

"Sorry, kid," Bat said, "our methods are a trade secret."

"I see," Spanner said. "Well, thank you for talking to me."

As he walked away, Delilah asked, "Why were you so mean to him? He's cute."

"Pinkerton just wants to find out how we did what we did," Bat said. "It irks him that we got something done that he couldn't. Let him wonder."

It had been almost a full week and not one more woman had been killed. Apparently, the killer had been true to his word. He'd left Denver.

"Maybe he did go home to England after all," Bat said.

"Let's hope," Clint said, "that he doesn't start doing over there what he was doing over here."

"There's still one question that needs to be answered," Delilah said.

"What's that?" Clint asked.

"Who stabbed Mr. Roper?"

"Yes," Roper said, shifting uncomfortably in his seat. His wound was still tender and painful. "I'd like the answer to that—"wait . . . a . . . *minute*!"

"What is it?" Clint asked.

Roper was looking out over the room and Clint followed his eyes.

"That's him."

"Who?"

"Him, that bulky guy who just walked in."

"No, no," Frank Quay said, "that's Royce Clayton. He's harmless."

"No, he's not harmless," Roper said. "That's the guy who stabbed me."

"The killer's follower?" Clint said, eyeing Clayton. "You're telling me that Clayton went down to the square to help the killer? To protect him?"

"I saw him around the square the first couple of days I was there, but I didn't think much of him. In the alley, I have to admit, he surprised me, and he was dressed in dark clothes. All that was missing was the cape."

"So he knew the killer?" Clint asked.

"Knew him, or had seen him," Roper said. "We won't know until we ask him, will we?"

"You got to watch out for the harmless ones, I guess," Quay said.

"How do you want to play it, Tal?" Clint asked.

"By the book, Clint," he said. "We'll take him to the police. I'll press charges against him for stabbing me. Maybe we can get something out of him about the killer."

"Maybe," Clint said.

"Let's go," Roper said.

Clint stood up.

"I'm coming," Bat said.

"Me, too," Quay said. "I always thought he looked

a little too harmless. Maybe it will take the four of us to bring him in."

"What about me?" Delilah asked.

Clint looked at her and smiled.

"You wait here. You and me have an interview to do before I leave tomorrow."

She stared at him and said, "Really?"

"Yes," he said, "really."

Watch for

THE WOLF TEACHER

166th in the exciting GUNSMITH series
from Jove

Coming in October!

Also look for a special GUNSMITH event
in October 1995!

**THE GUNSMITH GIANT:
THE LIFE AND TIMES OF CLINT ADAMS**

If you enjoyed this book, subscribe now and get...

TWO FREE

A $7.00 VALUE—

If you would like to read more of the very best, most exciting, adventurous, action-packed Westerns being published today, you'll want to subscribe to True Value's Western Home Subscription Service.

Each month the editors of True Value will select the 6 very best Westerns from America's leading publishers for special readers like you. You'll be able to preview these new titles as soon as they are published, *FREE* for ten days with no obligation!

TWO FREE BOOKS

When you subscribe, we'll send you your first month's shipment of the newest and best 6 Westerns for you to preview. With your first shipment, two of these books will be yours as our introductory gift to you absolutely *FREE* (a $7.00 value), regardless of what you decide to do. If

you like them, as much as we think you will, keep all six books but pay for just 4 at the low subscriber rate of just $2.75 each. If you decide to return them, keep 2 of the titles as our gift. No obligation.

Special Subscriber Savings

When you become a True Value subscriber you'll save money several ways. First, all regular monthly selections will be billed at the low subscriber price of just $2.75 each. That's at least a savings of $4.50 each month below the publishers price. Second, there is never any shipping, handling or other hidden charges—*Free home delivery*. What's more there is no minimum number of books you must buy, you may return any selection for full credit and you can cancel your subscription at any time. A TRUE VALUE!

A special offer for people who enjoy reading the best Westerns published today.

WESTERNS!

NO OBLIGATION

Mail the coupon below

To start your subscription and receive 2 FREE WESTERNS, fill out the coupon below and mail it today. We'll send your first shipment which includes 2 FREE BOOKS as soon as we receive it.
